# One Potion Five Oaths

Book 2 of the Wanderer Series

VERÓNICA GARCÍA

One Potion Five Oaths

Verónica García

ISBN (Print Edition): 978-1-66788-685-5
ISBN (eBook Edition): 978-1-66788-686-2

To my grandmother, Felisa, for her natural ability to bring joy and peace.

To the kind inhabitants of Earth, including humans.

# Up in Flames

The morning after reuniting with her long-lost twin Sister Darlith, witch Elath was beyond happy, "I'm going to send hummies to deliver the news to Alkefat, Shomes, and Milla. They ought to know Kiel is safe... and normal," she told Darlith and Kiel as they had breakfast.

Elath whistled, and three hummingbirds came to her side. Her dog Belugo also approached with a wagging tail, but she said to him, "Not you, Belugo. But I have treats for you, so stick around." Belugo, disappointed by her first statement, perked up after hearing the second.

The three birds hovered in front of Elath's face as she whispered, "Let your charges know what happened last night. Darlith is safe, and Kiel is a wizard instead of a giant. Go!" she said, snapping her fingers. The witch sounded very sure about this, yet, until that point, Kiel had not performed a single spell.

Elath gave Belugo the promised treats consisting of green beans and a bone that, at some point, had been part of a graceful antelope.

"Kiel, my dear," continued Elath, "it's time you put your powers to use. Show us what you've got."

Kiel swallowed his last bite of breakfast, wiped his mouth with a napkin, and thought about what possible thing he could try. Typical, he thought; nothing comes to mind when I have to think of something great.

"Relax," said Elath, "any little thing will do."

"You can do it," encouraged Darlith.

Kiel squeezed his eyes closed, held his breath, and tensed his body in a way similar to going number two—but he was out of ideas.

"It's best to let it... flow," explained Darlith, "just think of something you'd like to do."

Luckily, inspiration came as Kiel distractedly glanced at the enormous wooden chair he used to sit on as a giant. That chair belonged to his past and represented everything he wished to forget. He wanted to make it disappear, but not just that; Kiel wanted it gone with a bang. After focusing on it for a couple of seconds, the chair exploded into a million little pieces.

Fortunately, Darlith was ready for anything. She knew her son would not be able to control his powers just yet. With her broom, she launched a force field that held together the pieces before they blasted into them like wooden bullets. However, Kiel wasn't done yet. Even inside the force field, the pieces burst into flames, turned into a golden sparkle shower, and then dissipated into ashes. Darlith stopped the force field allowing the ashes to spread across the floor.

"That was... fantastically sloppy!" exclaimed Elath. "Congratulations, you're officially a wizard!" She showed Kiel the biggest smile. "I do have something you're going to need."

She entered the pantry and took out a broom Kiel had never seen before. Elath walked towards her nephew and said, "This is your broom, Kiel. You're finally able to use it."

Kiel took the broom in awe. Holding it with his left hand, he moved his right hand up and down the wooden handle, caressing it as if it was the most precious thing his fingers had ever touched. Kiel's broom was new, dark brown, smooth, and shiny, but at the same time it seemed to have the wisdom of a thousand redwood trees. It exuded wit and power, although in a raw state. Wild, untamed, and ready to go.

My very own broom, he thought, barely able to contain his thrill. This moment was undoubtedly solemn until Elath said, "Now swipe all the ashes, hon."

Darlith chuckled, nearly spilling her tea.

Elath kissed Kiel's head and added, "Love you."

As Kiel cleaned up the floor, he asked, "Where did this broom come from? I didn't know I had my own."

"Of course," replied Darlith. "When a witch is pregnant, a tree is planted. Many wanderers, not just family members, come and gift the tree with some of their best spells. The tree grows fast and is ready when the new wanderer is born. The best, thickest branch is cut, and a broom is made of it. Luckily, your Father Ottah, Alkefat, Elath, and I, together with a couple of family friends, planted the tree and performed the necessary rituals before Ottah and I traveled to the Foliage Islands to celebrate our first anniversary. This is your broom, Kiel—no one else's. It will help you control your energy. It is the most precious thing your Father passed onto you—Ottah hand-picked a seedling from the magnificent tree that has provided brooms for his family for generations. He wanted to ensure you were receiving the best broom he could provide. Elath requested that the tree be planted in her garden, where she could take good care of it. I can't wait to see what you're capable of, Kiel!"

"Indeed, the tree is right here in our backyard," added Elath. "It's your favorite tree, Kiel. The one you like to sit by, with the thickest base and largest canopy. You were naturally drawn to it."

"How come you didn't tell me before, Elath?" asked Kiel.

"I was waiting for the right moment. A time when you could use your broom. This is it, my dear."

About thirty minutes later, Uncle Alkefat flew in through one of the kitchen windows with one of Elath's hummingbirds on his right shoulder. He dismounted next to Darlith and hugged her tight and long. Alkefat's eyelids couldn't contain the tears that pooled.

"My sweet Darlith, how I've missed you!" exclaimed Alkefat. "I knew you were strong enough to survive Menof's rotten actions."

He turned to Kiel and said, "My dear boy, how I've longed for the day you became a wizard! The real you, at last!"

Finally, Alkefat hugged Elath and said, "You did it. You found Darlith safe and sound." Addressing everyone, he added, "I'm so proud of all of you. If only Valia and Leome could see you now... "

Valia and Leome were Elath and Darlith's parents and Kiel's maternal grandparents. Valia was Alkefat's little Sister. The mere mention of their names filled their faces with sorrow.

Elath's parents were renowned scientists that met a tragic end. Just six months after the twins were born, some forty years back, when they were finally ready to release their research into the world, a fast fire consumed them and all of their discoveries.

It was the first time in wanderer history that anyone had managed to carry a twin pregnancy to full term. Indeed, wanderers are highly individual beings. Even inside the womb, they refuse to share the mother's resources. The result is a party of one.

Somehow, Valia and Leome made it work against all odds. Doubling the chances for wanderers to survive was their dream. And twins were only the beginning. Triplets and quadruplets would have been the natural next step in their insatiable quest for knowledge. They had a real shot at saving wanderers from extinction.

But alas, it wasn't meant to be. Whether the fire was accidental or not hadn't been determined. No suspect was ever considered. Who would want to harm a peaceful couple while at the same time damaging their entire species? Such motive was inconceivable, and so would twin-ship be.

Uncle Alkefat raised the girls all by himself. It hadn't been easy, given how mischievous they were, but he wouldn't have traded it for anything else. Above all, Alkefat made sure Elath and Darlith knew who their parents were and how much their daughters meant to them.

Another one of Elath's hummies returned with a note from Milla. Elath read aloud: "So happy for all of you! Come to Crownfall Town soon so we can celebrate. Love, Milla."

Elath smiled, and then wondered whether Shomes had gotten the news yet. Lake Sangress was farther away than Crownfall Town, but her birds were quick. Begrudgingly, she forced herself to be patient.

But then, a strong feeling of dread came over her, together with a painful burning behind her left ear. The mark she'd given her four young human friends was in the same spot, and it couldn't be a coincidence. One of them was in trouble.

"Really?" she exclaimed, "I gave them the mark yesterday! I can't believe they got in trouble this fast and gravely enough to summon me!" She was visibly irritated. "This better not be a joke, or I'll take the marks away!"

But there was a problem—Elath didn't think the kids would ever need to use the mark, so she didn't give each of them a distinct one. She had no idea which of the kids was actually in trouble.

When she looked around her, however, she realized she could cover all the bases with Darlith, Alkefat, and Kiel. Elath wasted no time giving out commands.

"Alkefat, go to Tom's house."

"Darlith, check on Blume."

"Kiel, go to Veka's."

"I'll go visit Jake. That little rascal is the most likely of the four to be in trouble and be willing to prank me. Whatever you find, bring the kids here afterward."

A procession of brooms left Elath's kitchen through the window.

# Trouble

If Jake wasn't in trouble, he sure was going to be. On her way to Jake's house, Elath reviewed the wanderers' directives in her head, particularly the rules of engagement. Wanderers were prohibited from intervening in human affairs that involved grown-ups. It was permitted to interact with children, because adult humans never believed their children's magic stories. However, just like with anything else, some exceptions were considered. In cases where action was unavoidable, wanderers must make it look like their interference had been caused solely by humans.

"But human skills are so limited!" lamented Elath, speeding through the air.

Darlith and Kiel were the first to reach their destinations, since Veka and Blume's neighborhood was closest to Castle Marmelo. Each found a mature tree to land right outside the girls' rooms.

When Darlith looked inside Blume's open window, she saw the little girl fast asleep. Blume was so peaceful and cute; the scene made Darlith yearn for a little daughter. Blume wasn't in danger, but Darlith felt no need to go elsewhere.

From the tree, she whispered,

*Rose petals come to me*

*float up gently to this tree*

*bring all colors I command*

*pose them here in my hand.*

A stream of colorful rose petals ascended, and as soon as they touched Darlith's hand, she blew them right through Blume's window. Whenever Blume woke up, she'd find rose petals all over her room: on the floor, her pillow, bedspread, and other furniture. Darlith would wait for that moment to catch Blume's little face full of wonder.

Next door, Kiel peeked into Veka's room from the tree. He found her in bed reading a book about witches and wizards. Now and then, Veka would speak to the book, even yell, "That is so not true!" She kept on reading, and then said, "No way! You know nothing about them!" A few lines later, she got angry, "Oh no! They're not all ugly! I've met the most handsome wizard you could ever imagine."

Kiel flew to her windowsill to ask, "And whom would that be?"

Veka got startled, but that was much better than what she felt after: embarrassment beyond belief. No way would she admit Kiel was the most handsome wizard. A second later, she replied, "Well, Shomes, of course! Who did you think?"

"I was just wondering..." Kiel responded. "I was hoping it wasn't Fangas. If anything, he's gotten uglier through the years!"

Veka's puppy, Mint, repeatedly jumped by the window, trying to sniff who'd just come to visit. Alas, his short legs couldn't lift him very high.

Kiel smiled at the pup, and then got closer to pet it, "You know? Wanderers have written books about magic to mislead humans," Kiel explained. "Clever, if you ask me."

"What are you doing in my window, Kiel?" asked Veka.

"Oh yeah..." Kiel remembered. "One of your friends must have summoned Elath by using the ear mark she gave each of you. Since she couldn't tell who called her, she sent me to check on you. Darlith and Alkefat are also on duty."

"It wasn't me," pointed out Veka.

"I can see that. Still, Elath asked to bring you to the castle. Would you like to come?"

"Sure, but I need time to get dressed and let my parents know I'm going out. Will you wait?" inquired Veka.

"I will," said Kiel.

With that, he stayed put, right where he was.

Veka waited a few more seconds before asking, "May I have some privacy?"

"Of course!" he replied, and then flew towards the tree's top branches and faced the Green Ridge Mountains.

When Elath arrived at Jake's house, a man and a woman screamed at each other while a baby cried inconsolably. She stealthily approached the kitchen window to take a peek. Jake was curled up in a corner on the floor, holding his baby Sister and trying to soothe her while Jake's parents argued about money. The reek of alcohol filled the kitchen, even when a summer breeze gently moved the old, plaid window curtains. Mr. Hellington was heavily intoxicated.

As their argument moved along, Mr. Hellington became increasingly agitated.

"For the last time, Betty, where did you hide the money?" Mr. Hellington yelled at his wife.

"I didn't hide the money! I used it to buy food!" she yelled back.

Elath took a moment to consider her options. She could easily strike Mr. Hellington with a beam that would shut him up for good. This was, without a doubt, what she wanted to do. Fast, final, no mess, no fuss. The temptation to do so was rather irresistible. However, making it look like a human did it was problematic.

Next, she considered turning his speech into one that sounded like the screeching of a pig, but that, too, would be difficult to cover up. She had about another dozen ideas, from shrinking him down to a peanut-sized miniature man, to making him two-dimensional, to having him float away like a balloon that eventually popped, to gluing one hand to his mouth so he couldn't speak, and the other to his bottom for entertainment value, and everything in between. All those possibilities seemed rather exquisite to her at that moment. Sadly, none were humanly possible. Elath quietly ranted against the wanderers' rules of engagement and whoever came up with them.

Finally, she called a hummy and sent an urgent message to Alkefat.

Alkefat had gotten to Tom's house just a couple of minutes earlier. He'd found Tom in a barn milking a large, red-brown cow. The animals' smell and their recently cleared manure filled the otherwise airy space. There were no other humans around, so Alkefat walked right in.

"Good morning, Tom."

"Good morning to you, too, Alkefat. What a surprise! What brings you here?" Tom asked, happy to see him.

"I came to make sure you're all right. One of your friends summoned Elath through the power of the mark," explained the wizard.

"Oh no! Who was it?"

"I don't know," replied Alkefat.

"Was it Veka?" exclaimed Tom, horrified.

"I still don't know," chuckled Alkefat. "Whoever it was, he or she is in good hands now, so don't worry."

"Whose hands are with Veka, specifically?" insisted Tom.

"Kiel is with her."

"What? Why Kiel?" panicked Tom, struck by jealousy.

"Why not Kiel?" countered Alkefat, puzzled. "Calm down for just a second, will you?"

Just then, Elath's hummingbird came to Alkefat. The bird whispered Elath's instructions into Alkefat's hairy ear, and then the wizard asked, "Is your Father home, Tom?"

"I think he's taking care of the chickens. Why?"

"Because Jake's Dad is out of control and about to beat his wife and children. Elath will fill his path with obstacles to stall him, but another man should stop him and report him to the authorities."

"I'll get him right away!" cried Tom, running towards the chicken coup.

Tom's Dad, Mr. Wellson, became understandably alarmed by what his son told him. He ran inside his house to ask his wife, Sophie, to fetch the sheriff. She was to dispatch him to the Hellingtons' house as soon as possible. Indeed, this wasn't the first disturbance at Jake's farm, and the sheriff would know how to handle it.

Tom and his Dad rode on Mr. Wellson's horse to Jake's house as fast as they could while Alkefat flew beside them, hiding behind trees along the way.

When Tom's Dad stormed Jake's kitchen, Mr. Hellington had a baseball bat in his right hand and was about to swing it toward his wife. Meanwhile, Elath had come into the house through the back door and was in the family room with a direct view of Jake's Dad. She had had enough time to get very angry and comfortable with the idea of breaking the rules of engagement. After all, Alkefat was such a gifted cook; he should be able to concoct a potion for Betty Hellington to forget what Elath was about to do. Elath was done waiting and playing games. She was going to kill Mr. Hellington with one clean strike.

Mr. Hellington reminded her too much of Menof. The pain of Darlith's kidnapping was still very raw. A man praying on someone weaker, taking children hostage, or harming them without remorse would no longer be tolerated in her presence. Her eyes turned black just as they did when she confronted Menof, and the tip of her broom began to glow. The strike was ready to be launched.

"Last chance, Betty, give me the money!" threatened Mr. Hellington.

The house was messy, with furniture turned upside down and objects all over the floor, courtesy of Elath. Jake was still curled up in a corner protecting his frightened baby Sister.

"What's going on here?" yelled Mr. Wellson, storming into the kitchen. "Put that bat down at once, Henry! Are you out of your mind?" Mr. Wellson walked towards Mr. Hellington and, without hesitation, removed the bat from Henry's hand. This surprised Mr. Hellington because, until then, all his ire had been focused on his wife.

Elath took a deep breath and quickly left the house. With her eyes back to radiant green, she began to calm down.

As the sheriff's horses could be heard galloping in the distance, Elath and Alkefat retreated towards the trees and waited for the situation to be resolved.

"I was going to kill that man, Uncle," confessed Elath. "If you'd gotten here a couple of seconds later, Jake's Father would be dead."

"I understand, sweetheart. Menof has traumatized us all, and only time can heal such deep wounds," answered Alkefat.

Soon after, the sheriff handcuffed Henry while Betty, sitting on the front steps of their home, hugged her children and cried.

"How many drinks have you had today, Henry?" the sheriff asked.

"Let me look through my notes," Henry replied, unsteady on his feet. "Oh yes, not nearly enough!" he chuckled.

"Sounds like you still have some wits about you," commented the sheriff. "You're going to need them where I'm taking you. The other prisoners won't appreciate how much you reek of alcohol. When was the last time you bathed anyway?" he asked, not expecting an answer.

As the sheriff took Henry away, Tom's Dad approached Betty. "Betty, come to live with us for a while until Henry turns his life around. Sophie would very much enjoy your company. Tom can share his room with Jake, and you and the baby can have Nik's room. Let's ride this terrible storm together. We'll get through it."

"Thank you, Charles, that's a very kind offer and a great idea. I'll go pack a few things," replied Betty. "It isn't safe for us here anymore." She got up, her baby in her arms, and walked towards the house.

"Mom," Jake called, "I'm leaving with Tom. I'll meet you at his house later today. I love you."

"I love you too, honey." Betty went in.

Hidden inside a tree's large canopy, Alkefat told Elath, "See? Humans aren't all that bad. I think they do a better job helping each other than us wanderers! They have a much stronger sense of community. Since they don't have our powers, they're often forced to rely on each other. Sadly, most wanderers use their fierce independence to look out for themselves. There's much to be learned from humans, Elath. We would be wise not to forget that." Alkefat smiled.

"Oh, Uncle, always looking at the bright side," Elath shot back. "Let's get our boys and go home."

Tom and Jake searched the surrounding trees looking for Elath and Alkefat. A cluster of hummingbirds by one of them gave their location away. When Elath, her Uncle, and the two boys got to Castle Marmelo, Kiel and Veka were already there.

"What are you guys doing here?" asked Tom right away.

"We were waiting for all of you," replied Veka, petting Mint on her lap. Belugo was lying down, resting on Veka's right foot, as if he owned her.

Shortly after, Darlith flew in with Blume. The little girl was sleepy but perked up when she saw everyone gathered.

"First things first," said Elath. "I'm going to change the placement of your marks, so next time I know who, amongst you, is in trouble."

"No wonder it took you so long to come to my house, Elath," complained Jake, "I almost rubbed my ear off trying to reach you."

"It didn't take long. I had to make things look as if magic wasn't involved. It's not so easy, you know?" she countered. She wasn't going to let Jake's ingratitude get to her, but she wished he wasn't so grumpy all the time.

"Blume, sweetheart," Elath started, "you can keep your mark right where it's at, behind the left ear. Veka, I'll change yours to the right ear."

Elath approached Veka and swiped her hand behind Veka's left ear without touching it, and then behind the right one. She then turned to Tom and said, "Tom, your mark can go in the back of the head. Your hair will cover it." She walked towards Tom and swiped her hand behind his left ear first, and then the back of his head.

Since the marks had to be hidden to avoid unwanted questions, Elath paused to think. "Hmmm, where should I put Jake's?" she murmured. "Oh, I know! Jake's will be located in the right cheek."

"What?" asked Jake, covering the right side of his face with his right hand. "But then it will be visible! No offense, but I don't want a hummingbird in my pretty face."

The witch reached to swipe the air behind Jake's left ear, and then swiped on the right side of his bottom.

Tom, Veka, and Blume giggled. Darlith and Kiel smiled.

"Great, I'll be a pain in your butt!" Jake exclaimed.

"Tell me about it!" answered Elath. "Then I can be faster next time, isn't that what you want, dear Jake?"

"Well played, witch," answered Jake.

"Have you all had breakfast yet?" asked Darlith. "I'm going to prepare some food: scrambled eggs, bacon, and potatoes in spicy garlic sauce."

The kids were fond of the idea. Jake even clapped at the suggestion. "Finally, some good news," Jake said. He was starving.

While Darlith and Alkefat cooked, Elath sought a private moment to think. It had been long since anyone else prepared food in her kitchen. All of a sudden, she felt rather crowded. She wasn't used to being taken care of. It was a strange feeling, annoying even, but she understood she had to allow them to...at least for now.

She went to her room to lie on her bed, seeking a few minutes alone. Thinking of Jake's Dad, Elath hoped humans were able to bring Mr. Hellington back to health. As much as her relationship with Jake could be tense at times, she cared for the boy and wished him a bright future. Jake was both clever and resourceful, two things she respected. Those same two things reminded her of Shomes. I wonder if Shomes received my message, she thought. She closed her eyes and waited for the food to be ready.

# The Successor and
# the Snake

Back at Lake Sangress, Shomes woke up to the tickling of a hummingbird's whispers in his ear. The news that Elath and Darlith had managed to revert the damage Menof had caused Kiel was an excellent start to his day. Still, Shomes was there on a critical mission—to find Dazmian, and as of yet, he'd seen no sign of him. He wasn't ready to leave his post.

For hours he stared at the water with the type of laser-like focus capable of cutting a diamond, hoping for a clue as to Dazmian's whereabouts. The scenery had been undisturbed except for one minor slippery detail: a tadpole.

Shomes had watched the tadpole grow from almost nothing into something that swam with the enthusiasm of a rodeo bull. It swam first with its fish tail, and then its rear legs, and finally with the front ones. The tadpole changed direction every half a second, challenging Shomes' concentration with every turn. Yet the wizard's mind withstood the tadpole's frenetic pace that so shockingly contrasted against the seemingly slow passage of time. In reality, what should have taken eleven weeks from egg to frog, was happening in a matter of hours.

Finally, with a look of satisfaction, a shiny green-and-red frog jumped out of the water and sat right in front of Shomes.

RIBBOT, the frog croaked.

"Come again?" said Shomes, lifting his right eyebrow.

This time, instead of croaking, the frog spoke, "Why are you here?"

"Are you Dazmian?" asked Shomes.

"Oh heavens! I'm just a frog!"

"I see," replied Shomes. "I came to speak to Dazmian, the wisest of wizards. I don't suppose a talking frog could help me with that, could it?"

"Perhaps yes, perhaps no. What I'm sure of is that you can help me," stated the slimy creature.

"What would a frog such as yourself need help with?" inquired Shomes, more amused than surprised.

"I want wings."

"Haha," chuckled Shomes. "Now that I didn't expect. I was thinking more like a couple of roasted flies."

"I'll be happy to take those, too," said the frog.

"What kinds of wings are we talking about? The kind you eat, or the kind you fly with?" continued Shomes.

"The flying kind, of course. RIBBOT. But I'll take the other ones, too."

"So let me get this right. As an amphibian, you can live underwater and on land, but you want to explore the skies."

"Yeah, that's right."

"A little ambitious for a three-hour-old frog, don't you think?" pointed out Shomes.

"Don't worry about how old I am," contended the frog. "The question is, how long do I have left to live?"

"Good point... I suppose I could help you if it makes you happy."

"It would. RIBBOT."

"OK then. I won't give you wings, but I can certainly give you the ride of your life. Hop into my hood and hang on!" exclaimed Shomes.

As soon as the frog jumped into Shomes' hood, they took off on his broom to fly around the lake and its surroundings. They went so fast that only a blur could be seen—left, right, up, down, just as erratic as the tadpole in the water. Pirouette after pirouette until the frog begged Shomes to stop so he could catch his breath. "Please, please, I've had enough," the frog implored.

Shomes landed on the same spot they used for takeoff, and the frog slowly crawled out of the hood, slid to the ground, and stretched itself belly up on the sand.

"That was fantastic," whispered the frog, too tired to shout it. "Best. Flight. Ever."

"I'm glad you liked it. Would you like to go again?" inquired Shomes.

"No thanks. RIBBOT."

"Good," answered Shomes, lying next to the frog. He, too, looked at the sky rather pensive.

Another five minutes passed before either of them made a sound, but then the frog said, "I like you much better than Menof, you know."

At this, Shomes was surprised. "Did you say 'Menof?'"

"Yes," replied the frog. "I came out of the water yesterday to talk to him, too. First, he lied, saying he would help me, and then he tried to catch me for lunch! What an unpleasant fellow!"

"Who are you?" asked Shomes.

"I'm a little bit of this and a little bit of that. It's hard to say, really," was the strange answer the frog gave him.

"Peachy—I'll call you Fitz, then," answered Shomes, irritated by the ambiguity of the frog's response. "Did Menof try to kill you before or after you gave him that little speech?" he added.

"Before—Menof wasn't interested in who I am. His hungry intentions forced me to disappear back into the water."

"I see. Well, I don't know what I'm supposed to do with that, Fitz. Really, why don't you tell me how I can talk to Dazmian? I'm pretty sure you have something to do with him."

"But you have already been communicating with Dazmian," assured the frog. "I'm happy to say you passed Dazmian's test!"

"A test?" asked Shomes.

"Yes—a test of character. The same one Menof miserably failed," explained Fitz. "The question was whether you would help a homely frog for no other reason than being asked to do so." A smile covered the frog's face, remembering their recent flying adventure. "And now Dazmian has an important message for you."

"What's that?" inquired Shomes skeptically.

"Dazmian wants you to take Kiel under your protection and teach him how to be a wizard. Dazmian also wants you to show Kiel the Wanderer Library, including the Book of Deadlies and the Book of Deltas." Fitz paused to take a breath, and then said, "The problem is you only have a few days to do all this. Dazmian is dying."

"What? No!" yelled Shomes, horrified.

"I know you wanted the chance to learn from Dazmian, but you can do something better, Shomes. You can shape his successor."

"Kiel will take over for Dazmian? Why Kiel?" asked Shomes.

"For two reasons. First, Kiel's Father, Ottah, is a direct descendant of Dazmian. Kiel is Dazmian's great-great-great-grandson. As such, he has the potential for greatness. Certain traits and abilities get passed down from one generation to another. Dazmian hopes Kiel has both the ability and desire to see beyond the world that can be seen. Second, and most importantly, Kiel has spent the first sixteen years of his life going back and forth between good and evil. That experience puts him in the best position to understand the full spectrum of emotion. If one has to fight evil, it's best to understand it firsthand. In time, Kiel could even become wiser than Dazmian! Or at least that's what Dazmian believes."

"When you put it that way…" continued Shomes, "I guess it makes sense. My job, however, is to prevent anyone from learning Obslij. If that knowledge falls into the wrong hands, it would be extremely hazardous to the world."

"Yes, it would be, but these are dire times, Shomes. Did you know there are only a couple of thousand wanderers left in the world? And half of them are too old to reproduce even if they wanted to. Of those not too frail or old, many do not want the responsibility of caring for a family. If nothing is done soon, wanderers could be gone from Earth within the next hundred years! Without Dazmian's solution, I'm afraid the problem is irreversible—it's simply too late! Knowing Obslij can certainly be used for evil, but it can also be used for good. It's the only course of action left."

Frog Fitz paused to let Shomes come to terms with this information, and then added, "Dazmian has much trust in you and Kiel. If Kiel doesn't accept the challenge, witches and wizards will disappear—it's as simple as that. Dazmian is on the brink of finding a way to ensure wanderer survival, but his successor will have to finish the job.

"You know wanderers aren't supposed to live more than one-hundred-fifty years, Shomes. Dazmian is well past that limit, and because of it, he's not functioning at full capacity; he's hanging on by a thread! Damian and Kiel must meet. There must be a transfer of knowledge, or so much will be lost... Go now, Shomes; the sooner you start turning Kiel into a real wizard, the better," stressed the frog.

But Shomes still had doubts. He hadn't even been allowed to see Dazmian. Why should he believe any of what the frog was saying? Shomes turned to face the frog and stared deep into his black eyes, trying to figure out if Fitz was telling the truth.

The frog appeared to know precisely what Shomes was thinking. "Oh, you want proof? RIBBOT. I'm not enough proof for you?"

"Not at all," answered the wizard honestly.

"Fine!" exclaimed Fitz, as if his feelings were a bit hurt. "Dazmian wants you to grow your arm back. He says it's okay to learn from your mistakes and move on. The snake is dead; don't keep it alive inside you."

Shomes froze. He'd never told anyone that the witch that tried to steal the Book of Deadlies had come to him as a powerful snake.

Four years ago, when Shomes lived in a dark cave that he considered ideal for hiding the Wanderer Library, witch Loka tried to steal the books. Blinded by the desire to become the mightiest witch, she'd used a series of powerful incantations to turn herself into a deadly, seven-foot snake. With skin of bright red, black, and gold dragon scales, she believed herself invincible. She almost was—her specialty: the sneak attack. Hiding among shadows, she would patiently stalk her victims, waiting for the right moment to overtake them.

Shomes had heard word that a dangerous witch was after the Library. He'd been extra vigilant for days. On guard around the clock, he'd allowed no time to rest. But as time passed, he could no longer distinguish between the real and dream worlds. Sleep deprivation impaired his attention, alertness, reasoning, and judgment. Hallucinations began to hunt him. In trying to be the best guardian of all, he'd become useless to the cause. A significant oversight that he was unaware of. Shomes was quick to help others, but when it came time to ask for help, he just couldn't.

The fact that Shomes was somewhat of an orphan was likely the cause of his reluctance to seek help. His parents left him when they considered him old enough to survive—at eight years of age. It's not uncommon in wanderer culture to believe the best upbringing for a young wanderer is to fend for himself. The tough-love approach is relatively popular. But before Shomes' parents abandoned him, they ensured little Shomes knew he was in charge of his present and future. He shouldn't allow anyone to control him in any way. "When someone helps you, you become dependent on that person," Shomes' Father told him. "Dependence makes you weak. Weakness destroys you. You're your own best friend, son." These were his Father's last words to him. And so, asking others to join him in protecting the Library was unthinkable to Shomes.

Witch Loka had been watching Shomes spiral into such a confused state that she almost pitied him. Hidden in a dark area of the cavernous ceiling, Loka observed her prey's slow descent into madness. Unlike Shomes, she could use half of her snake brain to sleep while remaining aware of her surroundings with the other half. She was conniving yet patient, playing a simple game: psychological warfare.

As soon as Shomes closed his eyes, she'd send a bat to scream into his ear. A small rock would fall on him if he lay down to rest his head for a moment. When he looked right, a rat ran over his left side. If he looked left, some other incidental, like a raccoon, would bump up against his right side.

Eleven days went by until Loka decided Shomes was exquisitely ready. She would finally allow him to get the sleep he needed.

As Shomes fell into his deepest sleep, Loka gently slithered towards him with the confidence of someone receiving an award after an astounding victory. She'd devoted plenty of time to choose what part of Shomes' body she would bite first: his neck. Once she got to where Shomes was leaning against a rock, she lifted her head high enough to match his, and then stuck her tongue out to smell him. The tip of her red, forked tongue nearly touched Shomes' lips. When Loka's tongue went back inside her mouth to process Shomes' scent, she realized how much she liked him. Shomes smelled like a healthy, stimulating wizard covered in sweet freshly cut flowers—a remarkable scent after so many days in a cave without proper hygiene. It almost made her reconsider killing him. He would have made an excellent mate, she reckoned. Yet he was the only obstacle between her and the books that would bring her ultimate power.

Eliminating any positive feelings towards him, Loka lifted five of her seven feet above Shomes to gain altitude for her strike. She closed her slanted eyes and dived straight toward his neck. Her thick, sharp fangs belonged inside a great white shark's mouth instead of a snake's. Fortunately, even in a delirious state, Shomes too had smelled her vile stench, enough to make him move, just in time, four inches to his right and five inches up. Loka's jaws bit his left arm instead of her intended target.

Shomes cried as loud as a wizard could. His scream echoed throughout the cave, scaring thousands of hanging bats that flew away like a deafening black cloud. The pain was nearly fatal, but the adrenaline that rushed through his body brought back desperately needed focus. Having a huge snake biting his arm reminded him of lizards shedding their tails when caught. Just like lizards, he too could give up his arm for a higher purpose. And so he did.

The broom he held in his right hand became a razor-edged sword. He cut his arm first, and then the snake's head in two lightning-fast motions. Thanks to the swift separation of his limb, the snake's venom didn't have time to reach his heart.

He was safe for the moment, but needed to stop the bleeding. An incredible amount of blood is lost in seconds when a limb is cut. Quickly, he turned his broom brush into a melting-iron spatula and used it to burn his stump. He almost passed out.

Loka's reptilian body and severed head were putrefied within seconds, leaving two stinky piles of gooey, decomposed flesh by his side.

Shomes had to get out of there before adding the contents of his stomach to those piles. Shaken and feverish, he flew to Alkefat's cave to complete the healing process.

Alkefat's healing powers were known worldwide. "Mostly," the old man told Shomes later, "I just let you sleep for three days straight. You're the easiest patient I've ever had!" Alkefat chuckled.

In reality, Alkefat had worked tirelessly to save Shomes' life. He gave Shomes every healing potion he knew, plus a few new ones he created after sending Elath all over the world to collect rare medicinal plants. In the end, Alkefat wasn't sure what saved his life in all the elixirs he gave Shomes, but he was glad Shomes was alive.

"Now, can I help you grow a new arm?" the healer had asked.

"No thanks," Shomes had replied.

Even though Shomes saved the books by killing the terrifying witch, he still felt like he fell asleep on the job—which he did. But no one expects a wizard to have powers beyond his means. What he's expected to do, however, is to gather help if he can't handle a task on his own. Recognizing their limitations does not come naturally to wanderers, and the consequences can be devastating.

The shame of how close he came to losing the Library is the reason he chose to continue living without the arm, to ensure he remembered that some problems are bigger than one lonely wanderer. It had taken him a long time to learn this lesson, but he vowed never to risk failing again.

Still, the fact that Dazmian knew details Shomes had never spoken about was eerie. "How could Dazmian possibly know about the snake?" he asked the frog.

"He knows what he knows... and I 'knows' he knows a lot! Good luck to you, Shomes!" said Fitz, before disappearing back into the water in one swift jump.

Dazmian knowing what had happened that day with Loka was a relief to Shomes, as if someone had finally ended a nagging headache. Dazmian had even requested that Shomes move on. It was the greatest gift anyone could ever give him: the gift of forgiveness.

Shomes stood up, uncovered his chest, and grabbed a necklace with a small bottle and rolled-up parchment hanging off it. He opened the bottle with his right hand, drank every potion drop, and then twisted the top back closed. Unrolling the parchment, he murmured, "Let's see what good-old Alkefat has prepared for me." He began reading,

> *Grow left arm for I might*
>
> *need to fight*
>
> *stop a bite*
>
> *punch a dark knight*
>
> *stave off fright*
>
> *and even wipe?*

"Oh, the old rascal," Shomes chuckled.

Each time he voiced the spell, the arm grew nine inches. His hands and the tips of his fingers were completed by the end of the third round.

"Hoo-wee!" he screamed. "Oh, arm, how I've missed you!" Shomes cheered as he plastered effusive kisses up and down his new left arm. He then jumped on his broom and took off. It was time to drop formidable responsibilities onto Kiel.

While flying in Verdeval's general direction, he thought about what he could say to Kiel once he saw him, "Oh, hi, kid," Shomes practiced, "so glad you're finally a wizard. By the way, how would you like to...eh...dunno...save us all? You've been a wizard for at least eighteen hours—even if you slept through half of them. So what do you say, eh?"

# Confidential

When Shomes arrived at Castle Marmelo, he was still trying to figure out how to present things to Kiel. He'd wondered whether Darlith's run-in with Menof had been part of Kiel's destiny, or whether bad choices driven by greed were the only forces behind Menof's actions.

Perhaps there's a little bit of both—limited choices within a limited set of fates. Shomes pondered as he landed in the middle of Elath's kitchen.

"Shomes!" greeted Tom, Veka, and Blume enthusiastically. Blume ran over to him and jumped into his arms. Jake looked at Shomes, surprised.

Still holding Blume, Shomes exclaimed, "I wasn't expecting to find you all gathered here," before gently placing her back down.

As Shomes walked towards Kiel, he offered his right hand to the teenager. Kiel shook hands with Shomes rather awkwardly, since his former giant hands had never been suited to match normal ones. But after this simple gesture, Kiel felt like he finally belonged to the world of wanderers.

"I'm Shomes," the wizard introduced himself to Kiel. "We've met, but perhaps you don't remember—it's been a while.

You were just a little boy back then, and by little, I mean a mere ten feet tall!"

"I remember you," replied Kiel.

"Look at you all grown up! How tall are you now? Five feet eleven?" Shomes asked.

"Just about," agreed Kiel, "Funny, just this morning, I was told you're the most handsome wizard in the world, and now here you are!" Kiel smiled at Veka, but she looked away, not wanting anything to do with it.

Shomes, on the other hand, thought Kiel was referring to Elath, and the comment caught him off guard. Ever since Shomes met Elath, he'd never seen her show an interest in any wizard, even though she had several admirers.

Alkefat approached Shomes and embraced him. "Well, well, well... I can barely recognize you with two arms. You're so symmetrical!" The two wizards chuckled, and then Alkefat added, "I'm glad the potion I gave you worked."

"So am I!" agreed Shomes, and then murmured close to Alkefat's ear, "Although you should know I wipe with my right hand..."

"What's wrong with having other options?" Alkefat murmured back with a giggle.

"I certainly appreciate the thought," smiled Shomes. He scanned the rest of the room, looking for Elath, but only saw Darlith by the stove. He waved to her and complimented the aromas coming from the multiple pots and pans that ebulliently sizzled and simmered breakfast.

Just then, Elath walked in. "Shomes! Any news of Dazmian?"

Shomes looked at her as if he'd just seen a ghost. "Does Elath truly believe I'm the most handsome wizard in the world?" he wondered. He froze for a couple of seconds, struggling to remember why he was even there in the first place. But after regaining his composure, he went straight to the point. He'd envisioned having a private conversation with Kiel about what had happened at the lake, but perhaps it was better to share everything with everyone. Shomes sat down on a chair by the dining table and began recounting his bizarre experience with the frog.

As soon as Shomes finished talking, Blume stood up and walked straight to Kiel. "You have to help Dazmian, please! You have to help him!" begged Blume.

It's a marvelous thing, Shomes thought, to have a little six-year-old human around. How wonderfully easy it is for her to speak directly to Kiel's heart. Never mind that Kiel would be putting his life in danger. He'd become an instant target for wanderers who wanted his power. Never mind that if Kiel gave into his wicked side, he could destroy the world through new powerful Obslij incantations. Not for one second did little Blume consider that Kiel's life would become one of solitude because no one else would be able to match him.

Blume saw that without Kiel, there might be no more witches and wizards, no more magical poems, no more broom rides in the moonlight, no more delicious fruit, and no more turning imagination into reality. A sad world indeed. In her mind, this was only a choice between "Yes!" and "Heck yes!"

Kiel was hesitant, however. He didn't want to upset Blume and deflate her enthusiasm. He was proud to have been chosen for something of utmost importance. On the other hand, he had no idea what he was getting himself into. Worst of all, what would happen if he failed? He would never—ever—want to disappoint Elath.

Right across the room, Elath was distraught. Dazmian's request amounted to signing Kiel up for trouble. There was no way around it, yet she struggled to find one. Before she could say anything, the following words came out of Kiel's mouth: "Heck yes!"

"But Kiel," pleaded Veka, "perhaps you should take some time to think it over."

"It's his destiny," said Darlith.

"It's his choice," countered Elath.

"It doesn't matter," stated Alkefat. "Kiel's mind is made up."

Indeed it was. Kiel had watched Elath fight for sixteen years and was tired of standing by the sidelines. This time he would fight, too, regardless of whether he was ready.

"When do we start?" Kiel asked Shomes.

"Right away," Shomes replied.

"Before you two leave, know this," warned Elath. "If Kiel is in, so am I."

"And me," added Darlith.

"And me, of course," chimed in Alkefat.

"So are we!" yelled Tom, who with that statement, volunteered not just himself but all his friends, too.

"So be it. We're all in!" concluded Shomes. "See you in a day or two when Kiel completes the most intense training in wizardly affairs I can come up with. Time is of the essence."

Shomes got back on his broom, and Kiel mounted his. The rest watched them fly away with sorrow.

As Shomes and Kiel flew west, becoming two little specs in the sky, Tom noticed something else. Two other specs were flying south at great speed. After focusing all his attention on figuring out what they were, Tom screamed, "Pigeons!"

"What?" exclaimed Darlith, fearful.

"Where?" yelled Elath.

"Right there, flying south," pointed Tom.

As soon as Tom finished that sentence, Alkefat flew passed them, gently swiping Tom's blonde hair with his broom brush on his way out the window. He was going after the pigeons.

"It could be just a coincidence," stated Elath. "Unfortunately, it's more likely Fangas was listening in our conversation with Shomes. I'm afraid this is bad news indeed."

Alkefat returned a few minutes later. "I lost them," he lamented.

"We should assume Fangas knows everything," cautioned Darlith. "What should have been confidential will soon be public knowledge. Fangas is every bit as bad as his Brother Menof. Knowing I'm free, he'll think Menof is dead or in trouble. Either way, he will seek revenge."

"What are we going to do?" asked Tom. "Fangas may come after us."

"Not if we go after him first," answered Elath. "Are you ready for that?"

Darlith, Alkefat, and the kids nodded in agreement.

"In that case, I know just where to start looking," stated Darlith. "While I was under Menof's control, he took me several times to see Fangas. Even though I was blindfolded during the trip, there were several signs Menof couldn't hide from me.

"How many ways do you think you can sense an active volcano? I could smell it, hear it, and feel it. The roaring of an erupting volcano cannot be silenced with blindfolds." Darlith chuckled. "I enjoyed the many sounds of explosions, bursting bubbles, and gas propelled through volcanic vents. Then there are the red lights and shadows that faintly made it through the cloth that covered my eyes. The heat radiated was something to behold. The thermal energy penetrated my skin like no other heat source has before. Finally, a distinct set of smells, such as water vapor mixed with sulfur. All in all unmistakable.

"Islands are also recognizable by climate, humidity, smells, and sounds. Blindfolds didn't prevent me from smelling the ocean water or the fish markets. They didn't stop the noise of palm tree leaves swaying by the breeze. The local birds' songs were a clear giveaway, and landing on a warm, sandy spot is much easier on the knees! Menof enjoyed rough landings —as if conquering the site on touch-down," she lamented.

"If that wasn't enough," Darlith continued, "I recognized the typical dishes of the Papuaka Islands—so delicious, I wouldn't mind returning without the blindfolds. Once we get there, I'm confident we will be able to follow other clues that will lead us to Fangas."

"Well then, we shall go tomorrow at first light," decided Elath. She addressed the kids, "Will you be able to make it?"

"I don't see why not," replied Tom.

"I believe so," added Veka.

Blume and Jake nodded as well, and then Blume asked, "Can we have breakfast now?"

"Breakfast? It's more like lunch at this point," remarked Jake, starving.

"Of course!" exclaimed Darlith. "It's ready."

Everyone but Elath was hungry. Elath's appetite vanished when she heard Kiel would be put in harm's way. But with the smell of bacon in the air, the kids ate everything in sight.

"I'll give you a ride down the mountain and meet you there tomorrow morning," announced Elath.

# Full Moon

After a couple of hide-and-seek games, catching and releasing several lizards, and building a mud castle replica of Elath's home on a field half a mile away from Verdeval's central plaza, Tom, Veka, Jake, and Blume were ready to go home and rest.

Despite the threat Fangas posed, Tom was entirely preoccupied with Veka. He was sure if he didn't tell her how he felt soon, he might forever lose her to someone else. Was it too late already? A sickening sense of urgency overwhelmed him. He turned to Veka and said, "I'm going to walk you and Blume home tonight," hoping that, somewhere along the way, he might find a moment alone with her.

"Thank you. That'll be nice," replied Veka.

"That means I get to walk them too, since I'm sleeping at your house," pointed out Jake.

Indeed, consumed by the uncertainty of what Veka thought of him, Tom had forgotten about Jake's ordeal with his Dad. But talking to Veka in private would be very difficult if the four of them walked together. Could he get Jake and Blume distracted for a couple of minutes? Tom was out of ideas.

As they slowly strolled through the field toward Veka's home, a gigantic full moon lit their path and everything else around it. It had just gotten dark.

Tom looked at Veka walking beside him to his right. She glowed. Something about that particular moonlight gave her an additional aura of beauty. Her eyes sparkled like crystals in the sun. Her skin appeared as soft as velvet. Sensing his stare, Veka looked at him and smiled, and then looked back at the ground. She picked a wild purple flower growing by the side of the path and put it above her left ear.

Overwhelmed by her charm, Tom blurted out, "You look so beautiful at night, Veka."

"So does everyone else!" Jake exclaimed. "Surely Menof is a handsome guy in the dark," he chuckled—as did the girls.

"I suppose you're right," Tom admitted before giggling too. Having a moment alone with Veka seemed impossible. As soon as he got a little serious, Jake would make jokes about it. But then there was Blume...

"Tom likes you," Blume told Veka matter-of-factly.

Tom's heart did a summersault, and a rush of blood turned his face pink. Veka blushed, too.

"I mean, he 'likes likes' you," Blume continued, "like a Mom and a Dad like each other. You know? Kiss-kiss type of like," she said, blowing kisses in the air.

"No, he doesn't," replied Jake, somewhat disgusted.

"Yes, he does," Blume insisted.

"He does not!" Jake assured her.

FULL MOON

"He does, too!" yelled Blume.

"I know Tom better than you do," argued Jake.

"Then how come you can't see it?" replied Blume.

"Enough!" yelled Tom. "Neither one of you should speak for me."

"See? I told you he doesn't," concluded Jake.

"That's not what Tom said," chimed in Veka. "He said he should speak for himself."

With that, all eyes turned to Tom, "What is it then? Do you like Veka or not?" Blume demanded to know.

The topic had become a contest about who was right instead of Tom's feelings toward Veka.

"That is... a private matter," Tom answered.

"Of course it is!" countered Jake.

"A private matter Veka should know about, don't you think?" insisted Blume.

"Then perhaps you would allow me a moment alone with Veka so I can clear this up?" suggested Tom.

"Sure thing, Tom," agreed Jake. "Clear it all right up. Clear it up real good!"

Jake grabbed Blume's hand and gently but firmly dragged her farther along, just out of earshot.

Tom and Veka stood behind, facing each other.

"Well...that was something, wasn't it?" asked Veka.

"It sure was," Tom replied.

"Listen, you don't have to say anything," said Veka. "Blume and Jake can be silly. Competitive too!"

"But I do want to say something. I've been meaning to anyhow. I might as well do it now."

The silence that followed was awkward and seemed to keep Tom and Veka miles apart. Until Tom finally stated, "I do like you, Veka."

"I like you too, Tom, though I don't think that changes anything. You're my best friend. I wouldn't know what to do without you. Ever since I can remember, we've learned everything together. You've always been there for me," said Veka rather hurriedly, as if uncomfortable discussing the subject, eager to get it over with.

"And I always will be," said Tom calmly.

"OK, then. So nothing changes, right?" asked Veka.

"Whatever you want, Veka," replied Tom.

Veka's somewhat nervous reaction confused Tom a little. She's not ready to talk about this, he thought. At least Tom was in her heart, which was enough for him for the time being. He could wait, a lifetime if necessary. He would give Veka the space, time, and freedom to find him by her side.

Tom and Veka caught up to Jake and Blume just as a spooked black cat ran past them. An animated discussion about whether or not black cats bring bad luck filled up the time it took to get to Blume's house.

"I'm right, am I not?" Blume whispered to Tom.

"Yes, you are," Tom whispered back.

"Jake can be so thick sometimes," Blume added.

"You're right again," Tom replied, and they both quietly giggled.

The boys said good night to the girls, and then Tom and Jake headed home.

Walking towards Tom's house, Jake was happier than ever before. It was hard to believe his dream of living in the same place as Tom was coming true. Tom had what Jake considered to be a loving family. A family where all members sat down to have home-cooked meals together while talking about how their day had gone. A team where each player looked out for the other.

To Jake's family, all that mattered was in what mood his Dad was at any particular time. Jake's Mom, Betty, lived in fear of angering her husband. Her main focus was whether or not there was enough money to feed her children the next day. If that basic need wasn't met, any other aspect of life was inevitably overlooked.

But if I lived with Tom, Jake wondered, could I also become more like Tom? A happy kind of guy. Is life finally giving me a break?

Tom would often tell Jake to find the good side of things. Until then, however, Jake had refused because he didn't believe bad things could have a good side. But now, having his Dad in jail... he had to admit there was a good side.

When the two boys entered the kitchen, they found Tom's parents, Mr. and Mrs. Wellson, having a lively conversation with Betty. Indeed, Betty was smiling, laughing, and looking ten years younger.

Jake couldn't remember the last time he saw his Mom happy. Did I ever? he pondered. Yet there she was, chatting, giggling, relaxed amongst friends. Most of all, without fear.

Tom's Mom held Jake's baby Sister, Holly, while the two families had a delightfully peaceful yet animated dinner together. Indeed, Jake became a different kid—even if only temporarily. He was the kind of kid that enjoyed life thoroughly, miles away from the grumpy attitude he would often hide behind. For at least that night, there was no anger or resentment, just serenity, as if everything was going to be okay. Jake was safe, protected, and belonged to something bigger than himself. So this is how it feels to have a family and a home, he thought; I could get used to this!

The two boys shared Tom's room that night. But instead of playing as they might do on a regular sleepover, they were so exhausted they didn't even think about the dangerous trip they were going to embark on the following day before they fell asleep.

# The Pigeon's Hideout

The trip from Verdeval to Papuaka Islands was largely uneventful. Sadly, the same cannot be said of their approach to the volcano. About a dozen miles from shore, pigeons were already on the lookout.

Elath told the others to expect company. "I'm afraid we won't be taking Fangas by surprise," she lamented. Her priority was to land so the kids could get off the brooms, allowing her, Darlith, and Alkefat to fight unencumbered should they come across Fangas. But landing was a problem, given how many pigeons had gathered in the area.

"Let's move it!" Elath commanded. They sped up as the kids hung on tighter.

Veka rode with Elath, whereas Tom and Jake flew on Alkefat's broom. Little Blume wrapped her arms around Darlith's waist as if the witch was her new favorite stuffed animal. Darlith, in turn, was happy with this arrangement because she had grown fond of the littlest of the bunch.

Even though the kids had come to enjoy broom rides, it was hard for them to breathe upon reaching certain velocities and altitudes. In addition, the active eruption was polluting the air, making breathing harder the closer they got to the island.

Already in sight of the volcano, they shifted direction to avoid going over its massive crater. If they didn't hurry, things could become disastrous.

Suddenly, a large flock of pigeons came out of nowhere. So many of them made it hard to distinguish one from the other. Their movements were perfectly synchronized. Alas, the birds were headed straight for them.

"Uh oh," said Jake, who at that moment wondered why Fangas was any of his business after all.

Blume panicked and cried, "What are we going to do?"

"Don't worry, little one," Darlith comforted her. "I won't let anything bad happen to you."

But the pigeons were determined to surround them. No matter how the wanderers maneuvered, the birds followed. It would have been a beautiful display of the birds' masterful flight skills had it not been for the flock's malefic intentions. With each turn the friends made, the birds tilted in pursuit, and as they did, their wings reflected the sunlight acting like a million mirrors blinding their way.

Like the pigeons, the twins and their Uncle synchronized their flight patterns in a follow-the-leader fashion. Like an arrow-head, Elath flew in the first place, with Alkefat and Darlith slightly back to her right and left, respectively.

Elath dived. But down, too, the birds went. She then shot up, and up the pigeons rose. Next, she zig-zagged, and at this, the birds excelled! Speed was the group's best chance at getting away.

Flanked on all sides but one, there was only one way for them to go. Unfortunately, this would position them on top of the volcano's mouth.

Elath took a moment to curse Fangas. "Oh, Fangas! I will have your head on a spike for this, you wicked, vile, hideous, disgusting little pig!"

To that, the pigeons cried in unison, deafening their ears.

"Perhaps just curse him in your head next time," suggested Veka.

"That's a common occurrence, my dear," responded Elath.

The cloud of birds prevented them from seeing anything but forward. Even above their heads, the sky was covered with ash-colored wings. The birds were about to trap them by closing the only way out when Elath put all her might into increasing speed. Will we make it through? she wondered.

The pigeons' anger was both palpable and heard. OORHH! Came in a million different piercing tones. Under these circumstances, it was challenging to think, let alone strategize.

As Elath and Veka passed the fast-closing gap, their arms were brushed by dozens of harsh feathers.

"Haiyaa!" screamed Elath in victory.

"Yeehui!" was Veka's response.

But as they sped through the smoky atmosphere, they didn't hear any cheering from either their right or left sides. When Elath and Veka turned their heads looking for Darlith and Alkefat's brooms, they realized they weren't there.

"Where did they go?" exclaimed Veka as Elath made a sharp U-turn. Not a single pigeon was after them, either. The birds had stayed behind, forming a gigantic black sphere that engulfed their friends.

Tom and Jake screamed. Two long AAHHs reached Elath and Veka as the boys fell into what would be certain death. Their bodies didn't even have to crash; the volcanic explosions would vaporize them long before reaching a hard surface.

Blume also fell as Elath and Veka flew fast to catch the boys. Luckily, Darlith managed to set herself free from the aviary cage and went after her.

But the kids weren't the only ones falling; many dead pigeons dropped like black rain from the sky. Avoiding the lifeless birds made the rescue mission even more challenging.

Alkefat was killing as many pigeons as he could. The wizard was fully engaged in battle, launching beams of all colors in all possible directions. It was because Alkefat had all the birds to himself that the witches could attempt to save Jake, Tom, and Blume.

Since Jake was furthest down, Elath went after him first. "I can catch Tom right after Jake," she told Veka, but Veka remained silent, too worried to speak.

As Jake yelled, "HELP!" Elath went underneath him so he could grab her broom as he would monkey bars. Jake grabbed it—for a fraction of a second—before he continued to free fall.

"Scroutons!" yelled Elath before going after Jake again. "Really grab on this time," she commanded. "I don't have all day!"

Jake was getting dangerously close to the explosions, and Elath was sure there would be no more chances to get it right. Unfortunately, the smoke was so thick that it was hard to determine precisely where Jake was. Almost entirely in a gray fog, Elath again went underneath Jake. This time, however, Jake grabbed the broom as if his life depended on it.

Elath, with Veka and Jake sitting behind her, looked up to find Tom. Then Tom fell on top of them in a way that knocked Veka off the broom. Elath had gained two boys but lost one girl. She flew down, unable to see much of anything, and yelled, "Veka!" hoping Veka's response would give her a clue as to where she was.

Since Tom was still hanging off the broom precariously, the witch had to be careful not to lose him again. Breathing became more arduous, and the three of them began to cough. The heat generated by the volcano dried up their skin, and every fear-induced drop of sweat they produced quickly evaporated.

Elath wondered just how close they were to the explosions. "Don't worry, boys," she told them, "we're getting Veka back even if it's the last thing we ever do."

"I'd rather it isn't the last thing we ever do," replied Jake.

Finally, Tom sat on the broom securely, just as Darlith called, "Elath?"

"Veka's falling!" Elath yelled.

"I have Veka and Blume. They're with me," answered Darlith.

"Oh good!" Elath responded, much relieved. "Follow me," she added.

The Sisters moved far enough away to an area where they could see each other.

Elath had Tom and Jake move over to Darlith's broom, so the four kids rode with Darlith. A happy reunion indeed! Even if covered in ashes, coughing, and exhausted from the tension they'd endured.

"We should have moved you all to one broom earlier," Elath pointed out. "Darlith, take them to safety while I go help Alkefat."

"My pleasure," Darlith replied.

In the distance, Elath shouted, "You four need riding lessons!" while flying toward the pigeon's sphere.

As Elath approached the bird mass, she wondered how she and Alkefat would defeat so many pigeons. If they were to launch beam after beam after beam, it would take them all day to get rid of them. There has to be another way, she thought. She wished Shomes was there to help, because he always had good ideas. A moment later she exclaimed, "Of course! Falcons! The pigeon's natural adversaries. They will have a feast with these pigeons!"

Falcons were Shomes' bird companions. Shomes had taught Elath how to summon them in four verses. But he'd also told her that falcons were very independent birds, and they liked to know why they were being summoned before committing to a task. Elath was to recite additional verses after his, explaining why she needed them.

She closed her eyes, and then began:

> *Falcons of the vast sky*
>
> *on you today we will rely*

*Speed and predatory might*

*bring promptly to this messy fight*

*Enjoy all you can eat*

*don't leave a single pigeon treat*

*And though I sense Fangas is near*

*because he's uglier than an ass' rear*

*this will not be the cursed day*

*of that rotten wizard we fall prey.*

Just as she finished, hundreds of falcons began to arrive at the scene.

"That's what I'm talking about!" she cheered.

With falcons approaching from above, her chances of getting out of there unscathed skyrocketed. The falcons dived at a magnificent two-hundred miles per hour, making the eeriest and loudest, KEE KEE KEE, to the point where some of the pigeons decided, right then, to fly away, giving up Fangas' mandate to kill Elath and her companions. Unfortunately, many others remained, and those that stayed were the most determined.

Amid almost unbreathable air, sharp claws and beaks, broken feathers, and horrid KEEs and ORHHs, Elath finally saw Alkefat. The scene was hideous indeed, but there he was, with his strength, bravery, and all the years of service protecting his nieces. The old wizard had lost some of his shiny white hair to the raging birds. His neck and hands were covered in blood. Still, he looked resolute, focused, agile, and fully engaged.

Elath was immensely proud of her Uncle. He was more than her Uncle; he was her Father, just like Elath was both Kiel's Mother and Aunt.

Like a projectile piercing a compact ball of feathers, Elath flew to Alkefat's side. Together, they launched beam after beam to open a path big enough for both to escape. They succeeded.

"Let's leave the rest to the falcons!" yelled Elath to be heard over the battle noise.

"Agreed!" screamed back Alkefat.

Once out of danger, Elath and Alkefat took a minute to catch their breath, inhaling air no longer filled with smoke.

"The kids are safe with Darlith," Elath said with a smile. "You looked like a young warrior back there, Uncle."

"Who's to say I'm not?" chuckled Alkefat, cleaning his bloody neck and face with his sleeve. "Let's find the kids—resting is not my thing," he added with a wink. He was eager to see they were okay.

Elath and Alkefat navigated about ten miles northeast around the island, farther away from the smoke, before they spotted Darlith and the kids. They were sunbathing at a small, spectacularly beautiful beach with black-and-green sand. Blume stood out with her shiny, pink-sequined shirt. The sequins reflected the sunlight so brightly that boats could have mistaken her for a little lighthouse.

As Alkefat landed next to them, he asked, "Everyone OK over here?"

The kids nodded.

"At least we know this is where Fangas hides. No one commands pigeons the way he does," Alkefat remarked.

Darlith approached to tend to Alkefat's wounds.

"Oh, it's nothing, honey," dismissed Alkefat. "Don't worry about me. If you think a few silly birds can stop me, you're seriously mistaken." He smiled.

"Darlith, do you think you can lead us to Fangas' hideout?" asked Elath.

"I believe so," she replied. "Menof regularly met Fangas inside a cave. Fangas supplied Menof with the ghastly potion that took away my magic. I remember the surroundings had plenty of lush vegetation, so I would say the cave was on this side of the island instead of the arid, western side. We should head towards those mountains over there," she added, pointing towards the elevation behind her.

"Sounds good," said Elath, walking in that direction.

"I wish I could say the same," added Jake, "but if I don't eat something, I'm going pass out."

"You're hungry already?" Elath exclaimed, "Just how much does a twelve-year-old boy need to eat?"

"What can I say? Falling towards erupting volcanos has always made me hungry."

"I second that!" agreed Blume emphatically.

"All right, all right. We can eat some fruit on the way. There are plenty of fruit trees around here," conceded Elath.

"Like that apple tree over there," said Veka, pointing to a tree full of round, yellowish fruit.

"Good heavens, child!" exclaimed Alkefat. "That's the tree of death! The beach apple tree. The Manchineel tree. Don't you recognize it? The fruit resembles small apples, but everything about that tree is fatal: the fruit, the leaves, the white sap—everything!"

"Veka has a way of unknowingly picking poisonous trees," chuckled Elath. "I have come to understand that children are not taught about poisons in school, Uncle. Such a shame." She nodded disapprovingly. "Such a shame," she repeated.

"Well then, I'll be happy to teach you a thing or two," offered Alkefat. "Lesson number one: stay away from that tree!"

"Got it," acknowledged Veka.

They walked for about thirty minutes munching on bananas and mangos until Darlith announced, "We're close. I can feel it."

Just a bit ahead, they came across the entrance of a cave. As they were about to enter, Tom asked, "Wait a minute, what's the plan here? Do we have a plan?"

"Good question," answered Elath. "Given that Fangas just tried to kill us, I don't think we can play nice. However, we need information so we can't go in blazing hot either. We need to find out what he knows, his intentions, and who else knows about Kiel and Dazmian."

"That's not much of a plan, is it?" argued Jake.

"We go in and see what we're up against—that's the plan," stated Elath, not allowing further discussion on the matter.

They entered in a single file through a long, narrow, winding, dark passage. A few minutes later, however, a faint torch illuminated the way. Elath and Alkefat passed by the torch and kept going. Veka and Jake did, too. But as Blume passed by the light, the torch tilted down, and then back up.

Blume screamed, "AH!" moving erratically as if possessed by a lunatic. Her right sleeve was on fire.

Darlith, who was right behind her, wrapped her cape around Blume's arm and smothered the flames.

"Are you okay, Blume?" asked Tom.

"I'm not sure…" Blume replied, shaken. "Nothing hurts, but my favorite sequin shirt is ruined," she lamented. "Ruined!" she yelled, as her shock turned into indignation.

"Watch the torches!" Darlith warned. "They're out to get us."

Alkefat moved to the front of the line, trying to spot danger before anyone else got hurt. Every time he approached a new torch, he extinguished the fire with a flick of his broom. However, the torch would light up again a couple of seconds later, forcing Alkefat to put it out multiple times until they had all passed by it. Alas, when Alkefat put the fourth torch out, the ground underneath his feet hollowed, sending him fast down a spiral slide. Right before the slide dumped him into a spike-covered chamber, Alkefat transformed his broom's brush into a rake that attached itself to the slide walls.

While Alkefat hung by his right hand off the broom, his nieces' frantic calls traveled down and echoed off the cavernous hall, "Uncle! Where are you? Are you okay?"

"Never better!" he shouted back as his sweaty hand slid another inch closer to the end of the broom handle. "Fangas spent quite a long time sharpening these spikes," Alkefat murmured, making sure his nieces and the kids couldn't hear.

Fangas had added marvelous yet horrific designs to the walls and spikes of his deadly trap. Paintings of skulls, monsters, and ghosts adorned the walls, while the tips of the blades were carefully dressed in red paint meant to simulate blood.

Alkefat was intrigued and surprised despite being in such a dangerous situation. Is Fangas an artist at heart? he mused. How many rooms like this might we find if we stay long enough?

Alkefat created a ball of light in his left hand and sent it floating around the room to examine more details. The ball would give him a few moments to observe before losing its luminescence. The far corners of the room became visible, and to his astonishment, they were covered with spikes of hand-blown glass of all shapes and colors. They all had pointy ends that would ruthlessly penetrate the flesh of any fallen creature, but they were beautiful nonetheless.

"Crusty crickets!" he exclaimed, amazed by what he saw, just as his slippery hand slid another inch closer to Fangas' artistic abominations. Alkefat pulled himself up to grip the broom with both hands, and then transformed it again so he could fly on it. Slowly, he made his way up the twisty slide while uttering comforting words. "I'm coming up. You haven't seen the last of this old wizard yet," he giggled.

When Alkefat joined the others, he said, "You're not going to believe what I just saw. Fangas is an artist! He put so much thought into decorating a most frightening death chamber. He's got talent! Truly unexpected!" he concluded, excitedly.

"This time, you have outdone yourself, Uncle," replied Elath, "finding beauty in a space created to kill even the most innocent of creatures." She sighed as if reluctantly accepting her Uncle's ever-caring views.

"Maybe we should stop there on our way back so you can see for yourself," answered Alkefat. "Surely some of those paintings belong in a museum!"

"No thanks," was a joint response from his audience.

Elath wasn't going to spend more time in those perilous corridors of that haunted cave than necessary. "Of course, the way into Fangas' cave is booby-trapped," she said. "We have to be vigilant."

Elath helped the kids jump over the hole in the ground, and then cautiously moved along, putting out torches, and double-checking the ground's firmness before stepping on it.

The first chamber they got to was empty, cold, not too big, and a bit dark. The word "Greetings" was written in iridescent white paint across the far wall, yet somehow there was nothing warm about the space. Their eyesight barely adjusted to the low light when a muted explosion lit the room, and then knocked them all down to the ground. Fangas had deployed a bomb that forced them into a deep sleep. A hundred horns could have been blown directly into their ears and they wouldn't have awakened.

"Welcome! Welcome, everyone!" exclaimed Fangas as he walked in. "So glad you could make it," he chuckled, tiptoeing around their bodies. "Great timing!" he continued, cheering and rejoicing in his victory while none of them could hear. "My potion is just ready for you."

Fangas pulled a thin tube and a small funnel out of his cape. He also pulled out a bottle filled with brown liquid and placed it on the floor close to Elath's head. Kneeling next to Elath, he inserted the tube through her nose and pushed it down to her stomach. He then attached the funnel to the side of the tube he was still holding and poured one-third of the liquid into it while singing a made-up tune.

> *After an explosion*
>
> *I feed you my potion*
>
> *and when you wake up later*
>
> *please don't be a hater*
>
> *you know I must rule*
>
> *don't be such a fool*
>
> *submit to what's inevitable*
>
> *even if it's terrible!*

He repeated these steps with Alkefat and Darlith—without cleaning the tube first.

In this way, Fangas gave the Sisters and their Uncle the potion to neutralize their magic.

# The Missing Ingredients

The kids, Elath, Darlith, and Alkefat, woke up in a different, larger chamber. Each had their hands bound with string and tied to metallic loops affixed to the wall. Alkefat and his nieces were at least twelve feet apart from each other. The kids, however, were bunched together against a different wall. None of them knew what had happened; all they could remember was the explosion. They were confused, disoriented, and uncomfortable.

Fangas' cave wasn't cozy like Alkefat's. Numerous dead animals were lying around: rats of different sizes, a couple of bats, and plenty of cockroaches slowly decomposing. It was gloomy, smelly, and wholly uninviting. Fangas was in the center of the room, tending to a round pot about ten feet in diameter with a simmering brown liquid.

A feeling of dread overwhelmed Fangas' hostages.

"Okay, Elath," stated Jake, "now that we can see what we're up against, what's the plan?"

Elath looked at Jake in disdain; she wasn't in the mood for his witty comments. She needed to focus and assess the situation. "Shut up, darling," Elath admonished. She hoped to present a united front. She wasn't going to give Fangas the satisfaction of witnessing discord amongst them and possibly use it against them.

"Oh, please—do speak up!" intervened Fangas, moving closer to Jake. "Jake, is it? Unlike Elath, I'm interested in what you've got to say."

"Oh, yeah? Set us free, you crazy wizard!" blurted Jake, yanking on the string that attached him to the wall to no avail.

"Haha," Fangas laughed. "Of Elath's pets, you're the most amusing. Even though you threw up on me on our first encounter—and I most certainly haven't forgotten about it—I shall kill you last. Unless you'd like to work for me—we could do extraordinary bad deeds together."

"AAHH!" screamed Blume, terrified.

Fangas covered his ears with his hands and looked at Blume. "You, little monster, will be first to die. Surely my poor ears cannot withstand any more of your screams!" He shook his head as if trying to clear his ears of excess water.

"Over my dead body," chimed in Darlith.

"Aww. Would you listen to that?" teased Fangas, "Darlith has feelings for the littlest demon. Is she the daughter you will never have?" he giggled.

By then, Darlith knew she didn't have magic powers. The upset stomach and indigestion were symptoms she recognized well from the neutralizing potion Menof had given her for sixteen years. The vomit-like aftertaste—simply unforgettable.

"We have no magic," Darlith explained to Elath and Alkefat, so they would know it would be useless to try any spells. Darlith, too, tried pulling the string from the wall in vain.

Without powers, there was still one thing Elath could do. She launched a spit across the room toward Fangas, directly hitting his forehead.

"Bull's eye!" cheered Veka, unable to contain her delight.

Elath's spit leisurely slid down Fangas' nose while the wizard looked at it cross-eyed. "Impressive aim," he admitted, wiping his nose and forehead with his sleeve. "Still, I'm pretty sure I can survive a thousand spits." He laughed. "You're all quite comical, I must say. I mean, you didn't think any of you could actually hurt me, did you? That would be silly."

"What do you want with us?" asked Tom, tired of Fangas' chit-chat.

"You tell me. It's you who came for a visit. You that invaded my home. What do you want with me?" Fangas inquired.

"We came here to talk," answered Elath.

"Talk about what, exactly? The fact that you killed my Brother Menof? Is that what you'd like to discuss?" pressed Fangas in anger.

"As a matter of fact, yes. It was self-defense. He kidnapped Darlith, and you were his accomplice! Stop pretending you're innocent."

"Well, Elath, you should know that I loved my Brother very much," Fangas explained in a conciliatory tone. "He was like a father to me despite being only one year older than me. I will mourn his loss forever, and avenge it, of course." Fangas was, unhurriedly, walking around the pot, speaking as if thinking out loud. "However, I must admit Menof was a little short-sighted.

I mean, who would want to bother with your Sister when you could become the most powerful wizard in the world? His lack of ambition disappointed me greatly. Menof gave up the ultimate quest to dominate the world for one to dominate Darlith's heart. It doesn't get more stupid than that, does it?

"Instead, he could have been my partner for many years to come." He turned to Darlith with madness in his eyes, and added, "but he was obsessed with you! Menof chose to spend the last sixteen years of his life with you instead of his own family. Shame on him!" He shook his head disapprovingly. "What did he ever see in you anyway? You're as common as they come!" Fangas paused for a few seconds as if pondering something important before concluding, "There's this one thing Menof did right, albeit unknowingly."

"What's that?" Darlith asked.

"He killed your husband Ottah—a good thing indeed."

"Ottah was no threat to anyone!" exclaimed Darlith.

"Oh, but he would have been," Fangas countered. "If Ottah were still alive, Dazmian would have chosen him as his successor. Instead, Dazmian had to reach for a completely inexperienced wizard—your son Kiel."

"So you know about Dazmian and Kiel," said Alkefat, looking down in defeat.

"Of course I know! After I'm done with you, I'll find Kiel and finish him, too. And at that point, Menof and I will have been responsible for the demise of your entire family," he confessed with a grin.

"What do you mean by our entire family?" asked Elath.

"The only reason I tell you this is because today is the last day of your lives." He straightened himself up before delivering the nastiest blow. "It was I who murdered your parents, Leome and Valia."

The twin witches, as well as Alkefat, looked at him with a mix of disbelief and horror.

"I was only seventeen at the time," continued Fangas. "Still, it was easy because your parents were so trusting and unsuspecting. Good folk, some might say."

Darlith's heart stopped for a second as the awful news sank in.

Elath screamed, "You filthy rat! You will pay for this!" as she tried, unsuccessfully, to set herself free.

A tear ran down Alkefat's face. "But why?" he asked. "What could you possibly have gained from their deaths and the destruction of their research?"

"You see, Alkefat," explained Fangas, "while all of you wanderers do what you can to ensure that more wanderers roam the Earth, I want to be the only wanderer left on Earth."

"To rule everything," deduced Tom. "To be the most powerful creature alive."

"Exactly," nodded Fangas. "Would you like to hear how it all went down?"

No reply came, as his audience was struggling to assimilate the ghastly truth.

"Very well then," he began, taking their silence as a "yes." "Forty-six years ago, on a sunny summer day, when I was only eleven years old, I was sitting under my broom tree feeling rather lonely when I fell asleep. I had the most exquisite of dreams."

Then Tom remembered his pocket knife, a must-have for a practical survivalist like himself. I knew one day this knife might save my life, he thought. Tom turned to his left to whisper to Jake. "Jake, put your hand inside my right front pocket."

"What? No," whispered Jake back.

"Oh my goodness," growled Tom, under his breath, in frustration. He turned to his right to whisper to Veka, but this time, he chose his words carefully, "Veka, I have a knife in my right front pocket."

Needing no further explanations, Veka positioned herself a little in front of Tom, such that Tom's view was half Veka's back and half Fangas. Veka then moved her tied hands closer to Tom's right pocket and tried to get her left hand inside.

"What in the world are you guys doing?" asked Jake.

"Don't worry about it," replied Tom, barely moving his lips like a ventriloquist.

Veka was having difficulty turning her hand in a way that would fit inside Tom's pocket. She kept getting closer to Tom as she struggled, pushing him back a little.

"We're about to die, and you're playing some kind of game?" insisted Jake with incredulity.

"Be quiet and pay attention to Fangas," snapped Tom as quietly as possible.

Finally, Veka lifted herself on her tiptoes, and the angle was just right for her hand to slip into Tom's pocket. Alas, the pocket was pretty deep.

Fangas, who had just begun sharing his heinous tale with them, was immersed in his speech. "I dreamed I was the only wanderer left on the planet, the only being capable of magic. I didn't have to abide by the wanderers' directives or rules of engagement. I could do whatever I pleased. Everyone adored me. People treated me like a god. They came to me to ask for miracles. They bent over backwards to make me happy. They begged me to heal them. They even named their children after me — a whole village full of little human Fangas!" He laughed. "People loved me. It was a revelation. Who would have thought, to be loved, all you had to do was have all the power?"

"You're sick, Fangas, very sick," interrupted Alkefat, disgusted.

"Hold on, will you? I haven't even gotten to the best part," Fangas replied.

Fangas' horrible recount commanded everyone's attention except Veka's, Tom's, and Jake's. Veka's hand was still only halfway down Tom's pocket. She figured if she pushed down further, she might be able to get to the knife. As she pushed, Tom's pants came down a little, then a little more, and a little more still. Jake had a front-row view of three inches of Tom's undies. Still, Jake withheld his comments, but mostly because he was overwhelmed by Fangas' sordid tale and his friends' baffling actions.

"That day, I understood my purpose in life," Fangas continued, "and knew exactly what I needed to do."

As he went around the pot, Fangas' back was to the kids, and that's when Veka decided to make one final, hard push down. POP came a sound from Tom's pants as the button that held them around his waist flew into Fangas' potion, and his pants succumbed to the pull of gravity, covering his shoes instead of his bottom.

Suppressing laughter, which would have been quite disrespectful under the circumstances, Jake whispered, "Stay away from my pants, Veka."

Veka looked back at Tom and murmured, "Oopsies."

Tom was too embarrassed to do or say anything other than thank his lucky stars for wearing his favorite pair of undies. But he felt better once he realized Veka had the knife and was starting to cut through the string that bound her hands. Better to live without pants than die with them, he thought.

Unfortunately, Fangas was about to turn again and face them. The rotten wizard would undoubtedly find Tom's pants around his ankles highly odd.

As the recount of Fangas' horrid past continued, "Upon waking up from that wonderful dream, I was determined to make it a reality. For eight straight months, I worked hard, with very little sleep or rest, to find a way to eliminate all wanderers. It was a difficult and stressful time for me as I didn't know whether I could succeed. I studied wanderer reproduction systems in detail, and then developed a potion to sterilize wizards. The easiest part was how to spread it. Now and then, I'd go to Crownfall Town, to the very popular Farmers Market, and dump the potion in the kaleer. Wanderers have to have their kaleer!" Fangas laughed. "The effect of my potion on wizards is irreversible, such that if you drink it once, you won't be able to have babies. It was even more effective than I had anticipated! The birth rate fell almost immediately."

"Ottah was allergic to wheat and barley and, therefore, never drank kaleer," Darlith thought out loud.

"Ah," exclaimed Fangas, "that explains why you were able to conceive Kiel."

"Unfortunately," Fangas continued, "four years after I started spreading the potion, The Highest Wanderer Council decided to have your parents, Leome and Valia, work to find a solution to fight wanderer extinction. I couldn't allow that! When you and Elath were a mere six months old, I flew to the lab where your parents were conducting their research to create twins, triplets, and quadruplets. I went in..." Fangas was, once again, totally self-absorbed and looking at the floor. All it would have taken was for him to lift his head slightly and look towards the kids—but he didn't; he continued talking instead. "Your mother Valia was so sweet. She would have frowned upon your spit, Elath," lectured Fangas.

"Don't you talk about her!" yelled Elath.

"But wait—it gets better," Fangas went on as he slowly walked on.

Veka finished cutting the string around her wrists and began working on Tom's. It was then that Jake understood what was happening. Veka released Tom in less than a minute. Tom then used the cut string to hold his pants around his waist as Veka stealthily moved to sever Jake's string. Still pretending to be restrained, the three of them devised a plan to attack Fangas as soon as he turned his back on them again.

Fangas said, "After I greeted them, Valia gave me some cookies!" He laughed. "I told you she was sweet. Your Dad, Leome, asked what brought me there, and I told him I was interested in their research. I began asking questions about it, and they were happy to answer. It was incredible how much dedication and enthusiasm they devoted to the cause of preserving our species. If I hadn't stopped them, they might have succeeded. They casually mentioned they would make their research known to the Wanderer Council in a few days.

"Seriously," insisted Fangas, "if I'd been able to choose my parents, I would have chosen them. They were truly wonderful! We had a good time together, even if only for an hour or so."

Fangas was about to be in the correct position for the kids' attack when he decided to stop moving. "After I came out of the lab, I poured kerosene around the perimeter, set it on fire, and walked away. Your parents had so many explosive chemicals in their lab that they covered up their own murder! The kerosene traces at the scene were mixed up with oils, acids, peroxides, nitrates, and maybe even a bit of dynamite. Honestly, I'm surprised they hadn't blown themselves up with such an arsenal. By the way, you wouldn't happen to know who their supplier was, would you?" he giggled.

"You are worse than bad!" screamed Blume, crying.

"Can you believe Menof didn't even know I killed the scientists?" added Fangas, ignoring Blume's sobs. "That's what we used to call Leome and Valia—the scientists. It was all me," he stressed while pointing his thumbs at his chest.

"I have been terribly busy ever since. You don't know the half of it," whined Fangas, seeking empathy while standing in place. "All this time, I have been perfecting the potion to rid the world of magic powers, except mine, to neutralize the wanderers that are currently alive. Sixteen years ago, I created a recipe that works. It's the one you ingested while asleep moments ago. The problem is that its effects only last a few hours, which is not good enough. I have concluded that I'm missing some valuable ingredients." Fangas finally started walking again, "I'm now convinced I need human and wanderer flesh and bones to make it permanent. And this is where you all come in." He turned away from the kids. "I couldn't have planned it better myself—you're the missing ingredients! You will make the effects of my potion permanent!" He cheered with his hands up in the air.

Tom, Jake, and Veka launched toward Fangas just as Blume decided to close her eyes and try a spell. Even though the witches and Alkefat didn't have magic powers, Blume hoped some of their magic had rubbed off on her. She squeezed her eyes tight and uttered,

> Mean wizard, go away
>
> Set us free and let us play
>
> You're so ugly I don't like you
>
> Even if I stand behind you.

Tom, Veka, and Jake dumped Fangas into the potion so fast he didn't know what hit him.

When Blume opened her eyes, Fangas was gone, and her friends were free. Astonished, Blume saw Veka running to free Elath, Alkefat, Darlith, and finally her.

"I did it!" Blume screamed, "I defeated the wizard!" She jumped up and down enthusiastically.

"What are you talking about?" inquired Jake, confused.

Before Blume could answer, Darlith, who had heard Blume's spell, hugged her and whispered into her ear, "You sure did, honey. You saved us all."

Blume giggled, full of pride.

Alas, it wasn't wise to stick around to celebrate because Fangas was slowly climbing out of the pot. Judging by the excruciating grunts he was making, Fangas was in a world of pain. His skin blistered to such a degree that he was nearly unrecognizable. Fangas started a spell:

*Mortirum onecelot*

*killatas agorum*

But by then, the group was running out of the cave as quickly as possible. Since Fangas' spell had no effect, it appeared he had had a good gulp of his own medicine, rendering his invocation unsuccessful.

Once out of the cave, Elath and the rest of her party were blinded by the sun for a few seconds. They ran for a mile or so, seeking to put enough distance between them and Fangas. When they finally stopped to regroup, they bemoaned that they'd have to wait a few hours to regain their magic and fly off the island. The most important thing was to stay away from open areas where pigeons could spot them. Even though Fangas couldn't fly to them, he could still reach them by foot if he knew where to find them.

They walked for about an hour before settling close to a small beach where they could stay hidden by the trees. It was a beautiful spot for an improvised picnic.

"Darlith, we were lucky Ottah was allergic to kaleer. Kiel is alive today thanks to that," said Elath, trying to make sense of all the horrible secrets they had uncovered.

"Indeed," replied Darlith. "What about Shomes? Did he drink kaleer at Crownfall Town?"

"He never drinks on the job, and he's always on the job, so no, he's never drunk there that I know of," answered Elath. "What about you, Uncle? Did you drink kaleer at the Farmers Market?"

"Absolutely not, my dear; I always brew my own. When I turned eighteen, my Grandmother Sally gave me my Grandfather's recipe as a gift. She told me once I tried it, I would never be able to drink another type of kaleer, that there was simply no better one." Alkefat smiled. "She was right!" he added.

"Your kaleer is of high quality, exquisite taste with a hint of sweetness and perfect effervescence," remarked Elath with a wink. "I only hope you think us worthy of inheriting the recipe one day," she said, chuckling.

Alkefat smiled. "One day, my darling, one day..." But then Alkefat turned somber. "When I come to think of it," he said, "a number of my friends who came to me for kaleer have had children. Now I feel so stupid that I never made the connection. What kind of a scientist am I? I can't see the evidence when it's right in front of my face!"

"Oh, Uncle," soothed Elath, "don't beat yourself up; none of us saw it, not even Menof!"

"What kind of a wanderer has no idea that their Brother is the evilest creature in the world?" asked Darlith.

"It happens more often than you think. Evil characters can be quite nice to fool everyone around them," chimed in Elath, "Besides, Menof was no good either."

"So true..." agreed Darlith.

For the next few hours, they ate fruit, rested, played, and waited. Alkefat tried to make the various crawling bugs around him levitate, but it wasn't until after six o'clock that evening that a beetle got a good dose of befuddlement. The wizard lifted and moved the beetle around like a stringless puppet. He was overjoyed that his powers were slowly returning, and so would Darlith's and Elath's.

Alkefat selected a few more bugs to create a proper bug-puppet show. He pretended the little creatures were talking, uttering polite things like, "Oh, so nice to see you, Mr. Dung," and, "Have a nice day, Mrs. Droppings." The old wizard went on and on, lifting as many bugs as he knew synonyms for "poop." He had Mr. Muck, Mrs. Feces, Little Stools, Dr. Sewage, Miss Ordure, Scat Junior, Count Doo-Doo, and Professor Caca, all greeting and waving each other to the background sound of the kids' laughter. Even Darlith and Elath succumbed to their Uncle's silly antics. Alkefat's foolish "poopet" show effortlessly raised their spirits.

When the show was over, they all gladly flew back home.

Elath announced she would pick up the kids in the morning at their usual spot by the foot of the mountain to discuss the next course of action. Fangas was not only out of control but also determined to go after Kiel. She wasn't going to have any of it.

# Wrinkly as a Walnut

Kiel asked Shomes to allow him time alone with Dazmian. With the directions and map Shomes gave him, he had no trouble finding Lake Sangress. After landing, he strapped his broom to his back and pensively looked at the water. The lake exuded a chill serenity that Kiel happily inhaled into his lungs.

Suddenly, a frog hopped out of the water and touched down before him.

"Fitz?" asked Kiel, remembering the name Shomes used to refer to the frog.

"Follow me," answered the frog. "Dazmian's waiting for you."

The frog went back into the water, and Kiel had no choice but to follow.

At first, he noticed the water was quite cold, but he soon got used to it. With every step, he submerged another two inches of his body. After reviewing many water spells, he lamented that none would allow him to breathe under it. Still, he continued forward until the water covered him up to his lips. Alas, no sign of Dazmian yet. Annoyed, Kiel wondered whether Dazmian had become a fish. He took a deep breath and went all in.

What he saw was astonishing: the most beautiful coral landscape he'd ever seen. Brightly colored coral of all shapes, textures, and sizes mixed with sea creatures that did not belong in a freshwater lake. He could see far enough to know the lake would eventually be very deep.

Since Fitz was still signaling him to follow, Kiel continued forward until he could no longer hold his breath. But as he was about to propel himself back to the surface, underwater plants and algae tightly tangled his arms and legs, entrapping him. With the bit of oxygen left in his brain, he tried to understand why Dazmian wished him dead. Had this all been just a plot to kill him? If so, why?

The last image Kiel saw in his mind before losing consciousness was that of Elath, and the tears his eyes produced were the only saline drops in the lake.

Fitz looked at Kiel, who was gently being swayed by the water, like a baby rocked by his mother to sleep. His silky brown hair floated back and forth at the same speed as the plants that bound him to the lake floor. The frog stared at the young wizard, mesmerized by the sight of his smooth magical skin.

Fitz wondered just what kind of a boss Kiel would be. Dazmian had always been good to the frog, and knowing Dazmian's death was near, saddened him greatly. Immersed in such feelings, Fitz almost forgot Kiel ought to be waking up.

Kiel seemed either entirely peaceful or entirely dead.

Panicking, Fitz swam towards him and shook his left shoulder. No effect. The frog then tried tickling his armpit. Still no response.

Could it be that Kiel drowned? Fitz was horrified at the thought. Finally, the frog slapped him.

As logical as it is to think an underwater slap wouldn't hurt because the water would slow down the frog's hand significantly, the amphibian was so alarmed that he could pack a wicked punch.

Kiel woke up to an unpleasant frog's face attack. Still tied up and out of oxygen, he couldn't help but take a deep breath of water. To his relief, his lungs filled with oxygen instead of water. The plants weren't trying to kill him; they only showed him he could survive.

Once the plants released him, Kiel blocked Fitz's next punch with his left hand, and then swung his right arm to grab and squeeze the frog by his stomach. The frog's oval zero-like shape turned into an eight just as its tongue rolled out toward Kiel's nose at the muffled tune of a chain of bubble farts.

RIBBOTTT! complained Fitz.

"Why didn't you tell me I could breathe underwater?" gurgled a furious Kiel.

"Because I wasn't sure you could..." gurgled back the frog with difficulty. "Not everybody can—it's up to Dazmian. Besides, would you have believed me?" A little burp escaped the frog's mouth.

Kiel was squeezing all the gas out of the poor slimy thing.

"If it's any consolation," Fitz continued, "I was hoping you would make it."

"Why thanks, you little water rat," gurgled Kiel, angry after having died for a few seconds. "Now tell me, what am I doing here? Where's Dazmian?" he demanded.

"As I said—follow me," Fitz struggled to answer.

"You know what? Just point in the right direction; I'm done following you."

"Very well then," conceded the frog, pointing towards the far end of the lake.

Kiel released the stomach choke-hold on the frog, and they swam, side by side, in the direction Fitz had indicated.

They passed by many schools of small fish and even a few playful otters. Kiel didn't know what to make of a lake filled with a mix of ocean and freshwater flora and fauna.

Fifteen minutes later, they reached an underwater cave entrance on the other side of the lake. They dived in.

After two left turns and one right, they arrived at a very noisy chamber. Looking up toward the surface, all they could see was foam. The foam was caused by millions of bubbles caught in an endless cycle of being pushed down and fighting their way back up. They were under a waterfall.

They tried reaching the surface repeatedly, but the water-fall's crushing force pushed them down again and again.

Exhausted, Kiel paused to think. This was a humbling experience. As a giant, he hadn't encountered a natural force that could stop his physical strength. Then he realized that even after all the training Shomes had put him through, he was still thinking like a giant. A giant's first and foremost problem-solving tool is brute force.

"You're not a giant anymore! Stop thinking like one!" Kiel gurgled to himself in exasperation.

Standing at the bottom, he unstrapped his broom from his back and mounted it. In the blink of an eye, he propelled himself through the water to the top of the waterfall. Sadly, Fitz was left behind.

A crystalline river surrounded by the most beautiful meadows was feeding the waterfall. The sun was shining even brighter up there, which made the color of the grass and flowers incredibly vibrant—a sight that struck him as the most stunning he'd ever seen. He also noticed a reflective dome covering the entire area, which he figured hid this enchanted location from the air.

Kiel used one of Elath's spells to dry off, and then shaded his eyes with his hand to look around. He noticed a thick tree with a broad canopy about thirty feet away. And under the tree, a wizard.

The wizard was sitting on a rock and looking at Kiel with a broad smile. He looked ancient. His face, wrinkly as a walnut, was resting atop his hands, and his hands resting atop a warped and cracked walking stick. He was wearing an old, hooded dark-green tunic and a pair of worn-out sandals. His long hair was as white as snow, and his eyes were light brown with a hint of yellow. The strangest thing about him was that he was a bit translucent, as if he just came out of a recipe with one part wizard, one part ghost.

"Are you Dazmian?" Kiel asked, approaching him.

The old wizard nodded and softly replied, "My son, at last."

Dazmian spoke with difficulty as if infinitely tired because he was at least twice as old as he should have been.

The contrast between the two wizards was stark. Kiel's youth and energy levels were at their highest peak. His blushed cheeks and freshly washed skin only made his green eyes shine brighter. Kiel exuded vitality, fearlessness, and inexperience. Dazmian, however, looked frail but with the kind of inner peace that infected everyone around him. He exuded wisdom, compassion, and patience. Dazmian commanded admiration and love. Together, they appeared as two opposite ends of the same rope — the bookends of a journey.

Kiel sensed that Dazmian had much to say but little energy or time.

Dazmian slowly reached for Kiel's hand.

"I don't have much time, dear Kiel." Dazmian paused to breathe. "Please listen carefully. I found a way to increase the number of wanderers that roam the Earth," he breathed deeply. "All the answers are in my mind, but I can't remember them. You will have to go in and retrieve them."

"Go where exactly?" asked Kiel.

"Inside my thoughts and memories," gently whispered Dazmian. "My dear boy, you can do it." The old wizard smiled at Kiel again.

Dazmian had complete confidence in his great-great-great-grandson. Unfortunately, Kiel wasn't so sure.

"I'd be happy to, as soon as you show me how," replied Kiel. "Is there anything, in particular, I should be looking for?"

"Yes, there is," whispered Dazmian, taking time to utter each word. "A set of five magic Oaths and a recipe for a very important potion. The Oaths are written in Obslij, and you should find them bunched together. Both the recipe and the Oaths will be at the same location."

"What's the purpose of those things?" inquired Kiel.

"The potion will contain a dormant magic virus—once you prepare it. The Oaths will do two things: they will wake up the virus and bind the one who utters them to the wanderers' rules of engagement, way of life, and principles. Together with the Oaths, the virus can mutate humans"—Dazmian paused to inhale—"into wanderers."

Kiel was shocked. "You're going to turn humans into wanderers?"

"Heavens no!" chuckled Dazmian. "Although I hope some humans want to turn themselves into wanderers. It won't be easy to transition a human into a different species, but it's possible if you find the right kind of child."

"Have you tried it before on a child?" asked Kiel.

"Not the entire process...only parts of it here and there, over the years." Dazmian looked into Kiel's eyes. "But it should work," he smiled. "I'm sorry, son, I'd love to witness this transformation with my own tired eyes...it's what I've always wanted, but I'm afraid it cannot be. The research into creating a virus specifically tailored to humans, and coming up with the Oaths that would control its activation, was both complex and lengthy. In addition, the search for my successor took longer than expected. It wasn't until recently that you became a candidate. To my horror and dismay, the candidate before you, your Father Ottah, was unexpectedly murdered. I mourned his loss for a long time. You should know he was a fine young wizard. If your Mother, Darlith, hadn't healed you, I would have picked Shomes. However, Shomes has enough on his plate. He already has an important job to fulfill, one that he has gotten better at over the years. He is, finally, the perfect Guardian of the Library."

Just as Dazmian finished saying that, he disappeared, much to Kiel's surprise. Luckily, he reappeared a few seconds later.

Staying half-solid was draining Dazmian's energy. Nonetheless, the old wizard returned with a smile. "While inside my head, there are many other things you should come to know and understand. Meet me by that cave over there." Dazmian pointed towards the mountains behind him. "I'd like to show you something."

The old wizard disappeared again, and Kiel walked in the direction he had pointed. Dazmian was waiting by the entrance of a cave with tall ceilings. They went in.

In the center of the cavernous room was a stone table, with someone lying on top of it, seemingly asleep. When Kiel got closer, he recognized Menof's repugnant face. Instinctively, Kiel grabbed his broom and was about to shoot a deadly beam toward him when Dazmian got in between him and Menof. The old wizard didn't walk there; he slid through the air.

"He's no threat to you," Dazmian calmly explained. "Menof is evolving."

"Yes, he's going to evolve into a crispy pile of ashes!" exclaimed Kiel, moving to the left to avoid Dazmian and have Menof back in his field of vision.

Once again, Dazmian followed, "I appreciate your enthusiasm, young Kiel, but you're here for a higher purpose. Menof is going through an important process," softly added Dazmian. "He's reliving his life. This time, however, he's living it as every person he's ever encountered—everyone except Menof himself.

"He's experiencing the impact he's had on others. You can imagine that's not going to be any fun. At this very moment, he could be your Mother or yourself. The transformative power of this process reaches far beyond your angry beams."

Kiel looked again at Menof, but this time he got closer and focused on his face. Indeed Menof looked as if he was in pain. Still, Kiel felt his hand move towards a dagger he hid under his tunic.

"Think about it, young wizard," coached Dazmian. "Life is full of easy ways out, but easy doesn't mean it's the right thing to do. If Menof comes out of this activity transformed, he could have a tremendous influence on Fangas and other wicked wanderers. He could have more power of persuasion on evil characters than you could. If you kill him now, you will lose all that potential. So what's it going to be?"

After that, Dazmian disappeared again, leaving Kiel alone with his nemesis.

To say Kiel was upset would be an understatement. The mere presence of Menof was infuriating. Kiel was struggling. He started pacing back and forth, and then going around the table, weighing his options. While trying to control his anger and desire for revenge, Kiel couldn't help but notice Menof had a blackhead on his neck the size of a roly-poly. He got grossed out, and that yucky feeling strangely calmed him down. Suddenly, Kiel saw Menof in a slightly different light. He saw Menof as pathetic, perhaps even deserving of pity.

"I refuse to have Menof be saved by his disgusting black-head," Kiel declared, trying to regain his righteous anger.

This was yet another one of Dazmian's tests, Kiel thought. Damian wanted to find out if he could put the world's well-being before his own needs and desires.

But what if I can't? Kiel wondered. What if I kill Menof right now and leave? As Dazmian said, it would be easy.

Then he remembered Blume begging him to help Dazmian and save the magic world. He also remembered how Darlith remained Menof's prisoner for sixteen years to protect him, and Elath devoted her life to caring for him and finding her Sister. Even Uncle Alkefat put his scientific dreams on hold to act as everyone's father. All made sacrifices.

"But I want revenge so bad," Kiel murmured. Taking his dagger out, he approached Menof once again. Kiel's face was so close to Menof's that he could smell his warm, rancid breath. He backed up a few inches in disgust.

It was true that Menof appeared distressed as if having nightmares. The rotten wizard's face contorted in ways that signaled great suffering.

Regardless, Kiel placed his dagger on Menof's throat and whispered to him, "My Father Ottah deserved to live. You do not."

With that statement, Kiel was a judge and jury, but he couldn't decide whether to be an executioner.

He waited a few more seconds. Kiel expected Dazmian to stop him from harming Menof, but as of yet, no sign of the old wizard whatsoever. To Kiel's amazement, Dazmian was giving this choice to him entirely. He was touched by the trust his ancestor placed in him. Still, his hand was positioned just in the right place. A minor slip would end Menof's life.

After pondering his choices a little longer, he finally declared in frustration, "Oh, scroutons! The cockroach shall live."

Kiel moved away from the stone table, and Dazmian reappeared, smiling. "As I'd hoped, my dear son, you're ready," Dazmian declared.

Taking Kiel's hands into his own, Dazmian instructed, "Look into my eyes, then get lost in them."

"OK," replied Kiel, not knowing what that meant. It sounded strangely romantic, but something told him it was the beginning of a bumpy ride instead.

The staring contest began. Both wizards appeared hypnotized, and the journey through Dazmian's wise, old, magnificent mind began.

# Wise, Old, Magnificent Mind

A t first, being inside the old wizard's mind felt like a vertigo attack. Kiel's mind was spinning out of control as if his thoughts and Dazmian's mixed inside a tornado. Kiel's heart raced fast as he struggled to find some footing, something to grab onto. In hindsight, he realized he should have asked for further instructions on what to do.

Dazmian's soft, calm voice resonated inside Kiel's head, "Don't fight it, young wizard. This is the way to know someone's true intentions and heart. You'd be wise to remember it."

Kiel calmed down, and as he did, the speed at which their thoughts traveled slowed down significantly. Soon, he could distinguish between his ideas and those of his predecessor. The differences were significant. Kiel's ideas appeared fresh and intense, presented in a basic color scheme. Dazmian's, on the other hand, were shrewd, prudent, and came in complex colors. The most prominent dissimilarity, however, was their reach. Kiel's had to do with mundane, everyday things such as helping Elath take care of her castle and crops. Dazmian's thoughts were worldly in nature.

Dazmian's memories covered his remarkable and long life. Scenes where Dazmian was an advisor to world leaders, or a beggar in the streets of a busy town, feeding the poor at a shelter, teaching children how to read, playing dodgeball with indigenous tribes in faraway places, using medicinal plants to treat soldiers' wounds, and so on.

Kiel couldn't fully understand what he was witnessing. Was Dazmian a teacher? A healer? A leader? An activist? An explorer? A scientist? All of the above? It seemed as though Dazmian had lived a thousand lives, each of them different but with a common theme: compassion and tolerance. No matter what role he played, he was a humanitarian.

The old wizard had spent a good amount of his life amongst people. Perhaps more than amongst wanderers. Dazmian deeply understood humans, showing particular interest in the younger ones. He was especially fond of performing magic tricks to entertain children. Their expressions of wonder he never tired of. Nobody would have believed the tricks weren't tricks at all—it was the perfect cover for a wizard. Dazmian adored kids; he considered them a gateway into life's most profound wisdom.

Many of his memories had the unmistakable sound of children's laughter attached to them. Giggles, chuckles, titters, chortles, pearls, and shrieks of laughter all spread across millions of unforgettable impressions. Indeed, if someone were to ask Dazmian how he managed to live as long as he did, he'd happily reveal it was those jolliest moments that so vigorously fueled his engines.

"You will soon realize, my dearest son," came Dazmian's words inside Kiel's thoughts, "that if human children become wanderers, it wouldn't just be the children benefitting from this transformation by acquiring magic powers; our species would gain tremendously! Human children would bring a sense of community, an increase in empathy and cooperation, a cure for loneliness, and much-needed amusement and awe into our hearts. Hopefully, some of the human capacity to procreate will also transfer into wanderers as generations go by. Wouldn't all that be wonderful?" mused Dazmian.

Yet it wasn't only happy memories Kiel found. He saw Dazmian's suffering, too, caused by witnessing rampant wars, sick and hungry kids, and unrestrained greed and intolerance in a world growing in apathy as cruel leaders abused power. There was also the sinking feeling of dying before completing his dream to save his kind and pass the baton to a deserving wizard.

As Kiel dug deeper into this wondrous mind, he came across a particular section labeled "Survival." Inside, he found images of Dazmian working alongside Kiel's grandparents, Leome and Valia, guiding their research in a mentoring role. And that's when he saw a glowing, glittering treasure chest with an inscription, "The Five Magic Oaths." Kiel's skin was covered in goosebumps, 'I found it!' he thought with excitement.

He opened it, although he couldn't understand how he did it. Five beautiful pieces of paper bound together by a silver cord were stored inside. Each was written in glistening gold ink. Underneath, a small, black, leather-bound book. Kiel opened the book. The first page read,

*Wanderer Human Blend*

*Organic Ingredients*

*by Dazmian*

Dazmian's voice echoed, "Yes!" inside the walls of Kiel's brain, followed by, "I love you, young wizard. Bye now."

Kiel wanted to cry. His heart filled with sadness, but he managed to hold his tears. He felt something soft and furry on his right hand and leathery on his left. He realized he was no longer inside Dazmian's mind but back next to Menof's sleeping body. Dazmian was nowhere to be seen, felt, or heard—he was gone.

Kiel held the five-bound magic Oaths in his right hand and the recipe book in his left. Tears ran through Kiel's rosy cheeks; this time, he did nothing to stop them.

This is it, Kiel thought; I am the new Dazmian.

He'd been given the relay torch to conclude the most critical mission. The trouble was, he didn't believe himself fit for the task.

It doesn't matter, he told himself, whether or not I'm fit for it, I will get it done. His lack of confidence was replaced with stubborn determination.

Kiel looked at Menof, so harmless, defenseless, paralyzed, and deliciously vulnerable, on top of the stone table. Once again, he felt a pinch, an involuntary impulse to end Menof's life—he fought it.

"I'll deal with you later," Kiel told Menof.

As he left the cave, he turned around and added, "If I forget about you and you end up reliving your life for eternity…well, oops!" Kiel shrugged his shoulders and left.

Outside the cave, he stored the Oaths and the book inside his tunic next to the dagger, and then mounted his broom. From the corner of his eye, however, he saw a cauldron, a grill grate, a few measuring spoons, a serving spoon, and a couple of mugs on top of a rock—a parting gift from Dazmian. Kiel took the grate, put the utensils and cups inside the pot, and then went down the waterfall and into the pond below. He grabbed Fitz by the hand and shoved him inside the cauldron too. He then strapped the pot with a cord to his back and sped underwater in the broom.

"Are you going to eat me?" gurgled Fitz, visibly scared after settling inside one of the mugs.

No response came. Instead, Kiel offered a grin Fitz couldn't see.

At torpedo speed, Kiel, the spoons, the pot, the empty mug, and the frog-filled mug went through the lake to the site where he first landed at the Lake. Once there, Kiel told Fitz to guard the lake and do whatever was necessary not to let anyone get close to the hidden waterfall.

"Invoke plants, otters, or whatever you need to protect the cave entrance," Kiel instructed. "Who knows? There might even be sharks and orcas in this weird lake!"

Fitz was ecstatic Kiel had no interest in eating him, but then he remembered: "Dazmian's gone, isn't he?"

"Yes, he is," responded Kiel.

Fitz was flooded by grief.

"We're entering a new era, little frog, one in which I'm no longer mad at you." Kiel smiled and petted Fitz on the head. "We part as friends, and I deeply thank you for your service," said Kiel, extending his right index finger toward Fitz.

Fitz nodded and shook Kiel's finger with his hand. "Good luck, my friend," replied Fitz before retreating to the water.

A robin passed by, and Kiel called to it. He gave the bird instructions to deliver to Elath. She was to come to Lake Sangress with the children, Darlith, and Alkefat, to discuss important matters as soon as possible. Another robin was given instructions for Shomes to join as well.

Kiel then gathered two handfuls of sticks, a bunch of dry leaves, and a few logs. He closed his eyes and blew into the pile he'd collected. A beautiful pink flame rose from within the dry leaves, turning into a small, sustained fire. Kiel then placed the grate and iron pot on top of the flames and filled it halfway with lake water. Afterward, he looked for the long list of ingredients needed to prepare Dazmian's wondrous potion.

# Salt and Pepper to Taste

Gathered at Lake Sangress, Kiel asked Elath, Alkefat, Darlith, and the kids to sit around the gently simmering potion. He had important things to tell them. Even though he wasn't used to being the center of attention, he was proud to be surrounded by such loyal family and friends. Their lives had been turned upside down in just a few days, but they had all weathered the changes with remarkable finesse.

He couldn't help but be amused by all the expectant faces staring at him, including Elath's hummingbird Teal, who, perched on Elath's right shoulder, had his little head tilted to the right as if inquiring what all the fuss was about.

"You brought Teal with you," stated Kiel.

"Well, you didn't exactly tell us what's going on. I like to be prepared," Elath replied.

"Very well, then. Shomes sent word he's running late and that we should start without him," explained Kiel.

After going through the list of about eighty ingredients, Kiel was down to adding the last two, which he was holding in his right hand. The potion's recipe contained another recipe specific to creating the virus. It was lengthy and complicated, with at least ten incantations involved, but Kiel hoped he'd done it correctly.

"First things first," Kiel said to his attentive congregation. "What does 'salt and pepper to taste' even mean? Can't anyone write a proper recipe, for goodness' sake? Why do so many cooks leave such important ingredient quantities up to rookies like me? It doesn't make any sense! Can't they see it's in the 'salt and pepper to taste' step that most people mess things up?"

Elath wasn't the only perplexed member of Kiel's audience, but she was the one to ask, "Is this what you brought us here for, sweet pea?"

"No, no," replied Kiel, adding about one tablespoon of salt and another one of pepper to the pot. "Of course not. I'm afraid I have extremely sad news to convey to you," he stated in a severe tone. "Dazmian has passed away."

A cloud of sadness covered them as the terrible news sank into each of their hearts.

"I know you didn't know Dazmian personally," continued Kiel, "but I can tell you he was a marvelous wizard. I'm humbled by how much he knew and accomplished in life. He will be an inspiration to me for as long as I live."

After stirring the potion a few times, Kiel borrowed Darlith's scarf to protect his hands. He lifted the pot and moved it to the side to cool. However, he didn't put out the fire, to retain the cozy atmosphere.

"I have asked you all here, so you help me make the future a reality. As you might suspect, Dazmian made this world better in different ways. He protected us by trying to keep evil in check. He promoted compassion and fought intolerance and greed. He was a teacher, a healer, a soldier, and so many other things. He worked to improve small communities as well as entire countries. Yet his most significant accomplishment was creating a way for wanderers to survive.

"I have asked you here today to complete his ultimate goal. Together, if you wish, we can see it through." Kiel paused for a moment before explaining, "Dazmian developed a series of incantations capable of mutating humans into wanderers."

The kids reacted with a mix of whats, oohs, and aahs. Suddenly, Blume stood up and began jumping up and down. "Pick me! Pick me! Please, pick me!" she shouted, bouncing like a ping-pong ball. "I want to be a wanderer!"

Darlith giggled while Elath didn't know just what to make of it all. To her, it was crazy to think the kids were prepared to follow a wanderer's journey.

"Wait just a minute," Elath interjected, "these kids are too young to make such an important decision."

"This is true," Kiel agreed. "Ideally, they would be older so they could fully grasp the consequences of their decision. However, the transformation would be far more difficult if they were older, perhaps even unsuccessful. Their human brain would be less flexible, more set on its ways, and their immune system more apt to resist the changes," explained Kiel.

"No way!" yelled Blume, "I want to be a witch right now! I'm ready! I beg you, make me a magical poet!"

"Will we have to abandon our families?" asked Veka.

"Of course not," answered Kiel, "you can stay with your family for as long as you want."

Tom looked at Veka with eyes wide open. He couldn't believe she was even considering it.

"I'm in," said Jake, who saw this as an opportunity to, once and for all, set himself free from his troublesome family circumstances.

"This is going too far," cut Elath. "Tell me, Jake, why do you want to be a wanderer?"

"So I can turn my Dad into a chubby bunny, one that hops and hops and hops," he replied. Both Jake and Tom began hopping like little bunnies around each other. With their front teeth out and their hands together close to their chins, they made squeaky sounds each time they jumped, to the background chuckles of Veka and Blume.

"You see?" exclaimed Elath. "My point exactly! They will misuse their power. These kids aren't ripe enough—they need a few more Springs!"

"Their power won't develop overnight. It will be gradual, taking several months to complete. But as eleven- or twelve-year-old wanderers, they will be fully mature. Even Blume will be mature enough at six. I'm sure Jake will see the idiocy of turning anyone into a bunny." Kiel chuckled at the thought.

"No, I won't," murmured Jake, loud enough to provoke his friend's giggles again.

"The changes take time..." continued Kiel. "In addition, the incantations they have to recite are Oaths. They will have to abide by those Oaths and follow the wanderers' rules of engagement."

"Elath," intervened Darlith, "this is the way to the future. You can't stop it."

"I'm not trying to stop it, but we can't just dump such responsibility onto young humans such as these," argued Elath.

"You have nothing to worry about," insisted Kiel, "They will be mentored and watched."

"Oh, how much fun we're going to have!" exclaimed Alkefat. "I'm sure they won't be worse than the two of you when you were starting," he chuckled, pointing to the twins.

Elath took a moment to ponder. Things had changed so fast; she had to remind herself that Kiel was now a fully-fledged wizard. Not only that, he'd had access to Dazmian's wisdom, and Shomes had trained him. Elath looked into Kiel's eyes with joy. She trusted his instincts. If Kiel was confident it would work out, there was no good reason for her to object.

The kids looked at each other. Already Blume and Jake had opted in quicker than anyone expected. Tom and Veka, however, had yet to voice what they wanted to do.

Veka was pondering the possibilities. If she became a witch, she could make her dream come true. There would be no place in the world she couldn't get to, no corner unexplored. She could have lots of animals around her, just like Elath. She could surround herself with enchanted fruit trees and live in a castle. It all sounded pretty good. Except for the whole fighting bad guys part, Elath's life was one she fancied.

Yet something was holding Veka back; was it a betrayal to her parents? she pondered. Surely they wouldn't want me to change species just like that. Most likely, it would distance me from them. My parents would feel like they had lost their only daughter to something they wouldn't understand. The thought of how painful this would be to them almost made her cry. She was at a crossroads. Could she choose the future she wanted without crushing her parents' hearts into a million little pieces?

Tom was staring a hole through Veka. Of the four kids, he was the most comfortable in his skin. Even though he could see the advantages of becoming a wizard, he also saw the disadvantages. It was a whole other game, a much more complicated one. The stakes were higher, and every confrontation could be deadly. There was nothing wrong with his current life; there was much good in it. Thinking about all this, he realized he was almost one-hundred percent happy. There was only one small, tiny, minor little thing: Veka.

Tom believed he had a good understanding of what being human is all about. He figured life's an adventure where learning from mistakes is just part of the thrill. Life's about being there for friends, family, and needy strangers. It's about forgiving your imperfections and seeing the beauty even in ugly things. No one said it would be easy, but it did seem simple compared to a wanderer's life. There's nothing wrong with simple; it's how he preferred things anyway. While he understood why Jake would want to give up on his species and why Blume would like to fly like a butterfly to the tune of a few magical poems, he didn't think Veka needed to make any changes whatsoever. Veka was perfect the way she was. He wouldn't want to change a thing about her, nor would he allow anyone to do so unless that person was Veka herself.

As he looked at her and waited for a response, he knew that whatever she decided to do, she would be deciding for him, too. Whatever she chose would become his future as well.

Veka finally uttered, "I need more time to think."

Tom was relieved. At least she wasn't rushing into anything.

"Surely we would need more than two children, would we not?" asked Darlith.

"Yes," answered Kiel, "but Jake and Blume will be the first to try."

"You mean, we're guinea pigs," concluded Jake.

"Exactly," cheered Alkefat. "In this case, being a guinea pig is a great opportunity. You'll be pioneers in the most exciting research anyone has ever heard of."

"Can any child become a wanderer?" asked Veka.

"Good question…" Kiel answered. "There's one minor requirement that needs to be met."

"What's that?" asked Jake.

"I have to go inside of you," replied Kiel.

"What? No!" exclaimed Jake. He imagined himself trying to swallow Kiel as a snake swallowing an alligator. "I'm sure you don't taste good," Jake blurted out.

"What?" exclaimed Kiel. "My goodness! You don't have to eat me. I have to go inside your mind, Jake. I have to know your thoughts and your heart. I'm sure you can understand I have no intention of turning rotten children into rotten wanderers. That would be disastrous. Only those of the right kind of heart will be allowed to transform. Do you think you're of the right heart, Jake?"

"Sometimes...I suppose..." Jake replied truthfully. After all, if Kiel was going to see his thoughts, there was no point in trying to hide his flaws. All would be revealed—to Kiel, anyway. He was willing to pay the price if the reward was to be able to run away from his Father.

Perhaps I could even help Dad recover, Jake thought. I could put a spell on Dad's taste buds such that alcohol tasted like rotting fish. He might stop drinking, then. Or I could turn alcohol into water before he drinks it. Or I could have it cause an allergic reaction such that his whole body would look like he had chickenpox; he continued daydreaming. With so many possibilities, Jake's mind was already filling with the fantasies of a new life with magic.

"You can get inside my brain if you want to," stated Blume. "I have nothing to hide."

Her statement made everyone laugh, much to Blume's bewilderment.

"First, I will go inside Blume's mind, and then Jake's," explained Kiel. "After that, we can all recite the Oaths together. They're harmless without the potion."

"If Blume and Jake are completely decided, they can drink the potion. If Veka needs more time, we can reconvene tomorrow morning."

"Tom, have you decided what you'd like to do?" inquired Elath.

"No. I need more time, just like Veka," Tom replied.

"Very well, then. May we proceed?" Kiel asked, looking in Blume's direction. "Are you ready, Blume?"

"Absolutely," Blume responded.

Kiel took Blume's hands and explained, "You're going to feel dizzy at first, but if you calm down and relax, things will settle down fairly quickly. I promise it won't take long."

The first thing Kiel saw once inside Blume's head was butterflies. Tons and tons of butterflies of different colors and patterns, flying in all directions. Suddenly, the wings of the butterflies turned to pages. Pages upon pages Blume had scribbled scrabbled on over hundreds of papers. Every one of them had a different poem in it. Kiel reached for the pages, grabbing three. The first one read,

> *Roses are reb*
> *Violets are blue*
> *Be my frend*
> *And I'll love you.*

The second one read,

> *Wen you are stinky*
> *stay away from me*
> *go take a bath*
> *and bring me dack tea*

The third one read,

> *Leafs are green*
> *Lilies are yellow*
> *You eat a bean*
> *I eat a mashmellow.*

Despite the spelling mistakes, Kiel got the gist of it. He then saw memories of Blume playing with her parents, rolling around the grass, or being tossed up in the air by her Dad. They had a peaceful, happy life together. Kiel then came upon the image of Blume hiding inside a closet, eating chocolate, seemingly without her parents' knowledge. On another occasion, Blume stole a few coins from her Mom's purse. She had told herself she had borrowed the coins and would return them later. But later, she never returned them. A couple of other instances showed Blume struggling with right and wrong. At times she chose to share toys with other children. Other times she snatched toys away from those same children after they found no interest in her poetic whims. Whatever the case, there didn't seem to be any dark corners to be explored. Blume's thoughts presented themselves as what Kiel thought to be the normal development of a young and bright human mind. Overall, Kiel concluded, her heart followed a path of righteousness, just as he suspected.

"I've seen enough," Kiel declared, breaking the link between him and Blume.

"Did I pass?" Blume asked.

"With flying colors," Kiel assured her. He turned to Jake and asked, "How about you, Jake? Are you ready?"

"As ready as I'll ever be," Jake replied. He had reluctantly accepted to be mind-probed. Despite detesting the idea, the potential reward was too good to pass up.

Kiel wondered what he was going to find inside Jake's mind. It was indeed a flagrant invasion of privacy. Did he have the right to do so? Yet how else was he supposed to determine whether he should allow them to have magic? He wondered. He had no answer to that for the moment; therefore, going inside Jake's deepest thoughts, fears, and desires was the only way to find out.

At that moment, it dawned on Kiel that Dazmian, too, had gone into Kiel's mind. It wasn't just an expedition to find the Oaths and the potion; Dazmian had cleverly gotten into Kiel's dreams and ambitions. Why wouldn't the process go both ways if one knew how to do it? Kiel was sure the wise old wizard had also vetted his mind, and Kiel didn't even know it. He smiled at that realization. Had Blume paid any attention to any of Kiel's thoughts? Or did she have to be a wanderer to see inside his mind? He decided to test that theory.

"Blume, I wonder," Kiel started, "if you had to guess what my deepest fear is, what would you say it was?"

Blume looked at him, confused at first. She then looked at her friends as if asking for suggestions. Tom suggested, "Menof?"

"Good guess," replied Kiel, "but that's not it."

"Giants?" put forward Jake, making everyone laugh.

"Funny," acknowledged Kiel.

"Your biggest fear is failure," proposed Veka.

"Good one," admitted Kiel, "but not quite it either." It struck him that Veka was more intuitive than he expected, and she'd come very close to the truth.

"I got it!" screamed Blume. "Creepy-crawlies!"

"Excellent!" exclaimed Kiel. Blume confirmed she'd had no access to his thoughts with that answer. Relieved, Kiel could proceed with Jake.

"OK, Jake. Here we go," Kiel followed the same steps he used with Blume.

Jake's mind was a lot more complex than Blume's. Their age difference meant Jake could see more of life's complexities. Not a lot of black and white, but many shades of gray instead. The general atmosphere in Jake's mind was rather gloomy, and Kiel didn't particularly like it there. When he began getting images, he realized they were mostly of two kinds: happy and somber. The happy ones had to do mainly with Tom. Times when they hung out together, especially when Jake felt like he was part of Tom's family. The sad ones all had to do with Jake's Dad: his drinking, lousy temper, yelling, the occasional beating he gave Jake, and the overwhelming neglect Jake had endured.

Unfortunately, Kiel had to go deeper into those feelings if he was to know Jake's heart. Kiel saw how many times Jake had considered running away from home. How much resentment he harbored against his Dad. But the ultimate question was still unanswered: was Jake capable of evil?

If anyone should know, it was Kiel. He, himself, had battled a powerful thirst for revenge. The urge that told him if he could get rid of Menof, the wound Menof had inflicted on him would heal. Luckily, Dazmian had shown him that if you eliminate one evil character, another one pops up. Dazmian had taught him, in the brief moments they shared, that the way forward is not to kill but to transform instead.

Jake heard Kiel's voice in his head: "Transformation instead of elimination. Figure out if anyone or anything can help your Dad find his way back to your family. Otherwise, let him go. If you hold onto hate, you'll never walk the path to healing."

Something then happened inside Jake's mind. Something that allowed Kiel to see cheerful memories of Jake and his Dad together some years before Mr. Hellington started drinking. Memories that felt like they'd been buried under five tons of cement. As if Jake never, ever wanted to think of them again because they hurt so badly.

Kiel realized how much Jake actually loved his Dad and how desperately he needed him. With that, he felt he'd seen enough. Jake's despondent, shadowy attitude was just an expression of profound grief. It was the only way he found to cope with the loss of his Father to alcohol addiction. There was no real evil in Jake's heart. He was a boy dealing with neglect, trying to hang onto normalcy through Tom's friendship and family. It was unlikely Jake would choose a crooked path, even if that's what Jake wanted people to think. Jake was protecting himself against rejection by rejecting other people first, as if that could make things any better.

Once Kiel broke the link between him and Jake, he was surprised to see tears running down Jake's cheeks. Jake reached out and hugged him.

"Thank you," said Jake, looking up at Kiel.

"No problem," Kiel replied.

Jake was thankful to remember how much he wanted his Father back. Perhaps Mr. Hellington wasn't a lost cause after all. If there was a chance his Dad could be saved, then Jake was determined to take it.

"You passed the test, too," Kiel added. "Congratulations to both of you," he said to Blume and Jake. "Now to the Oaths. I will translate the meaning first, so you know what you're about to swear by. Once I say it in Obslij, you will repeat it after me. If you do not swear by these Oaths, you will not be allowed to have magic. Any questions?"

No questions came.

"The first Oath means you will not harm except to defend yourself or other victims of evil. It goes beyond that; it implies respect for all living things."

*Iyo timik duran comethas net lamis telas vilean.*

Everyone, kids and wanderers, repeated.

"You will exercise restraint and mercy to the best of your abilities."

*Iyo shilab faritas sethas cusan mias.*

"You will keep your nose out of human affairs when-ever possible."

*Iyo neris banas litas humenas extas welas.*

"You will speak the truth as you see it."

*Iyo zurub megines cuffit solenas.*

"This last one is the equivalent of 'live and let live,' a call for tolerance."

*Levit undy cummas levithean.*

Once everyone finished repeating the last Oath, Kiel cheered, "Bravo! We're one step closer."

# Concealed
# Metamorphosis

It was time to drink—at least for Jake and Blume. Kiel handed each of them a mug filled to the top.

Jake moved his mug to toast Blume's. "Cheers. See you on the other side," he told Blume with a wink. He proceeded to drink the potion in big gulps without pause.

Blume watched in astonishment, as did everyone else. She waited a minute before drinking from her mug, expecting Jake to become some kind of monster. Nothing happened.

With all eyes on him, Jake exclaimed, "That's it? I feel the same, look the same." He lifted his right arm to sniff his armpit and declared, "and phew!—smell the same."

"Give it time," insisted Kiel.

Blume slowly began drinking her potion, one small sip at a time, as everyone stared at her. Jake grew impatient, and said, "Just drink it already so we can get on with our business."

Blume sped up and finished with a loud burp.

"Well, come on!" said Alkefat, "I'll take Jake over to those trees and see what kinds of things he might be able to do. Darlith, would you like to bring Blume and do the same?"

"Absolutely!" Darlith exclaimed, excited.

As the four of them got up and walked away, Kiel told Elath, "There's something I'd like to show you. A loose end, shall we say..."

"You know what I do with loose ends—I end them," stated Elath.

"Yeah, well, this one's a tad complicated..." insinuated Kiel.

"Where to?" Elath asked, eager to understand what he was talking about.

"Follow me," instructed Kiel, mounting his broom.

The two of them, plus Teal, flew above the lake toward the far mountains, disappearing in the distance.

Veka and Tom were left alone by the fire. Veka welcomed this moment of intimacy because she wanted to talk to Tom about the transformation. It wasn't like him to keep so quiet about it. Veka trusted Tom completely and listened to his counsel. Such a big step could not be taken lightly.

"Shall we go after Jake and Blume?" suggested Tom.

"In a minute. First, I want to talk to you about something," replied Veka.

Meanwhile, Alkefat kneeled next to a wild yellow flower in the woods and put his hands around it without touching it.

"We need to start you with something simple, like accelerating a flower's growth," he told Jake. Alkefat then whispered to the flower,

> Flow and glow
>
> Below the rainbow
>
> Bloom I bestow
>
> Growth undergo
>
> throw a show
>
> and not just so-so.

With those words, the flower opened up and displayed the brightest and largest bloom it could deliver.

"Your turn, young Jake," Alkefat announced.

Jake kneeled. With his hands, he surrounded a flower much like the one Alkefat enhanced, and then uttered,

> Glow and mow
>
> Flow from below
>
> Show a potato
>
> Grow in a row
>
> and not just so-so.

No effect.

"Were you even paying the slightest bit of attention?" Alkefat asked in disbelief.

Blume and Darlith, who had been closely watching, giggled freely.

"Was I supposed to memorize it?" Jake complained. "I thought my incantation was just as good as yours."

"Not even close!" Alkefat exclaimed, half-amused, half-flabbergasted.

Suddenly, the dirt around Jake's enchanted flower began shaking and cracking as if coming to life.

Blume screamed, "Look! Something's happening!" pointing to the ground.

One by one, in a perfect row, three apple-sized, malformed, grayish, warty potatoes popped from the little plant's roots. The flower itself didn't look so happy.

"Would you look at that!" cheered Alkefat incredulously. "A wizard you are! No one said you would be a good one!" he chuckled.

"Woohoo!" exalted Jake, jumping around the flower-potato. He kneeled and picked one of the ugly tubers so he could show Tom later. Jake looked at his creation as if it was the greatest accomplishment in the history of humankind. He loved that potato. Moving it closer to his lips, he planted a big, noisy kiss on it.

Then a voice whispered into Blume's ear, "Forget potatoes. Where can we find a butterfly bush?"

Blume asked, "Why do you need a butterfly bush, Darlith?"

"I don't," replied Darlith. "Why do you think I need one?"

"Because you just told me," answered Blume.

"I did not, my darling," insisted Darlith.

"Well then, who did?" asked Blume, puzzled, looking at Alkefat and Jake.

"I don't think it was either one of us," answered Jake.

As they all looked at each other confused, two lime-sized butterflies flew around Blume's head. One of the butterflies was bright blue with black along the edges of the wings. The other had a reddish, orange hue with white and black circles on its wings that resembled eyes. Both appeared happy to be orbiting Blume's head.

Suddenly, Darlith grasped what was happening. "It appears these two butterflies are talking to you, Blume. You can understand them. What a delightful skill to have!"

"Yes! Yes! Yes!" yelled Blume, unable to contain her joy. "Don't worry, butterflies; I'll help you find food." Blume grabbed Darlith's hand and dragged her farther into the woods, searching for a butterfly bush or something her new insect friends would like to eat. Amused, Alkefat and Jake followed.

"The butterflies can have a potato if they'd like," Jake commented as he trailed behind.

"They don't like them," answered Blume.

Not too long before Jake added three monstrous gray potatoes to a pretty yellow flower, Elath and Kiel arrived at the cave where Menof lay in a state of hyperactive dreaming.

"No!" yelled Elath, shocked to see Menof, "It can't be!"

She readied her broom to fire the most powerful beam she could muster.

"Wait!" commanded Kiel, "let me explain."

"What is there to explain?" Elath asked, agitated. "Menof isn't dead. I'm going to fix that right now."

"Don't you trust me, Mom?" asked Kiel.

His question melted Elath's heart. For the most part, Kiel referred to her as Elath, but he'd call her Mom now and then, especially in times of need. Since Darlith was finally back in their lives, Elath didn't expect Kiel ever to call her 'Mom' again.

"Of course, I trust you more than you could ever know," she replied.

"Then allow me to explain," Kiel insisted. "Dazmian put Menof in this state. Menof is undergoing a conversion. A kind of deep cleansing, if you will. By reliving his life as every being except himself, he's experiencing all the pain he's caused others. Dazmian believed this process would change Menof in a way that would serve humanity."

"Dazmian was quite the optimist, wasn't he?" Elath remarked. "Perhaps because he wasn't subjected to Menof's malevolent actions."

"Dazmian was indeed an optimist, but he was also wiser than us. We should honor his legacy by at least giving him the benefit of the doubt. We need to see this process through," stated Kiel.

"Then why did you bring me here, Kiel?" inquired Elath. "You knew I'd want to terminate Menof."

"I brought you here because of four main reasons. First, I don't know how to wake him up. Second, I don't know when to wake him up. Third, I figured if he woke up and was still evil, we'd be two against one. And fourth, because I trust you, too."

"In that case, here's what I think," began Elath. "The only way to find out if this process did any good is by waking him up. We need to restrain him. Let's do it right now."

"But how can we wake him up?" asked Kiel.

"There's a couple of strategies I'm willing to try," replied Elath with a wicked grin on her face. "Are you ready?"

"I guess...," answered Kiel, unsure what to expect.

Elath and Kiel tied Menof's feet with a rope they found at the cave, piled with other tools. They turned him to the side and tied his hands together on his back. Finally, they bent his legs by the knees and tied Menof's feet to his hands. Menof was restrained. After, Elath shut Menof's greasy nose with one hand and waited.

"You plan to smother him?" asked Kiel.

"Smothering him is plan B," replied Elath.

"What's plan A, then?"

"He might wake up. Cutting off the flow of oxygen may trigger his brain to rouse," hypothesized Elath.

"And if he doesn't?"

"If he doesn't... perishing in his sleep is a compassionate way to die. Certainly better than he deserves," asserted Elath.

"Didn't we all just swear by Dazmian's Oaths not to harm other than in self-defense?" pressed Kiel.

"I'm simply trying to wake him up, as you asked me to. If he dies, it truly would be an unintended consequence."

Kiel was making Elath nervous with all his questions. "Would you please relax for a second?" she begged him, "and get ready. We don't know what we're going to be up against when and if he does come back to consciousness."

Unable to breathe, Menof's body started to shake. At first, with little quivers. Then medium shivers. Finally, wide trembles almost sent him off the table. Elath had difficulty hanging on to his slippery nose, but she was determined. She resorted to using both hands to ensure that no single oxygen atom made it through.

Just when they thought Menof wouldn't make it, his mouth and eyes opened simultaneously, and he took the deepest breath he could.

Elath let go of Menof's nose and quickly put her concealed dagger to his throat.

"Don't you move," Elath warned Menof.

"How could I? It looks like I'm all bundled up," answered Menof, taking big breaths and coughing a little.

"You sure are. Don't even think about attempting to escape," cautioned Elath.

Menof relaxed a bit. He looked at Elath, then at Kiel, and said, "I'm sorry."

"Sorry for what?" inquired Elath, pushing the dagger closer to his throat.

"For everything. I'm afraid I've been quite terrible not only to the two of you but to your entire family. I'm certain you cannot forgive what I've done. It's unforgivable," concluded Menof.

"You're right about that," nodded Kiel.

"Elath," continued Menof, "go ahead and kill me. I don't see how I could live knowing what I know. The things I've done. The kind of life I lived."

With the dagger firmly in a deadly position, Elath looked at Kiel and said, "I'm not sure I'm buying this, Kiel." She couldn't tell if Menof was telling the truth. What if it was all an act? What if his words of repentance were all just a pile of horse manure? she wondered.

"We can only know by seeing it through," declared Kiel. "Just because he's awake doesn't mean we have to trust him. We have to watch him at all times."

"Agreed," said Elath.

Elath moved the dagger away from Menof's throat and cut the rope around his feet instead. She then instructed Kiel to release Menof's hands while she readied herself to strike if he tried anything she didn't like.

Just as Elath released Menof's feet, Tom got closer to the pot to smell the potion.

"Hmmm, it smells delicious," he proclaimed, "although I'm quite hungry, many things might smell good right about now."

"Tom," said Veka in a serious tone, "I don't know what to do. I'd love to have magic, but my parents would be very sad."

"Are you asking for my advice?" inquired Tom.

"Yes. I know you understand me, and I value your opinion."

"Well... I don't think you need magic. I mean, look at all the things you can already do. You're great! I don't see why you'd want to change anything about yourself."

"Thanks, Tom. But think of the possibilities. Traveling any place in the world would be so easy!"

"I can see that. It would be thrilling for sure... but it could also be quite dangerous," Tom pointed out. "Think of how many times we almost died since we met Elath. That kind of life is not for everyone. Besides, you can still see the world as a human at a slower pace..."

"You're right, of course," agreed Veka, "so we shouldn't transform, right?"

"I didn't say that...I can't make that choice for you. But you don't need to be a wanderer to do what you want in life."

Veka had a pensive expression on her face, so Tom asked, "How do you know your parents would be upset about it, anyway? If this is something you want so badly, it might surprise you to know how understanding they can be. Just like when I talked to your Mom about the puppy, she didn't want you to have a puppy, but she understood how much it meant to you."

"I'm pretty sure they wouldn't like this. I would often be gone, exploring faraway places."

"You could limit your travel depending on how much your parents could handle," Tom suggested.

Even though Tom didn't want Veka to become a wanderer, he supported her no matter what. He wanted her to be happy.

"I don't want to upset them," continued Veka. "I'm their only child, you know?"

Just then, someone came crashing down from the sky as if a gigantic grasshopper had landed next to them.

"Fangas!" cried Tom.

Fangas' face was filled with madness. His eyes were full of dark anger, and his skin was covered with blisters. A foamy, white substance was pouring out of his mouth as if he had rabies.

"Ahh!" yelled Veka and Tom.

Fangas grabbed Veka's hair with his right hand, and Tom's hair with his left, and then dunked both of their heads inside the potion-filled pot.

"Do you like taking baths in potions, you little monsters?" roared Fangas. "Is it yummy in there? Drink as much as you want! The more, the better!"

Fangas had no idea what the potion was for or what it did, but he didn't care. These kids had dumped him inside his steaming hot concoction, and he was returning the favor.

Tom and Veka tried to free themselves by pushing away from the pot with their hands. As they desperately attempted to lift their heads to breathe, they took several gulps. Luckily the potion was warm instead of hot.

Fangas was deceptively strong. He kept both kids submerged despite their efforts to liberate themselves. "Do you think it's funny or polite to dump someone into a simmering potion?" yelled the mad wizard. "I want you to know what it feels like." He laughed.

Fangas could not have imagined that the potion he had just forced Tom and Veka into had the opposite effect as the one he had prepared. Where Fangas' potion took magic temporarily away, Dazmian's enabled it for good. This is not what Kiel intended to happen after they all recited the Oaths. Kiel hadn't even vetted Tom and Veka by looking into their minds.

In his fit of rage, Fangas had unknowingly decided their future as fully fledged wanderers. It's unclear whether he intended to kill them, but he was mad enough to do irreversible things that changed people's lives forever.

Luckily, Shomes launched a beam toward Fangas' head before landing on top of him just before Tom and Vera passed out. Fangas was knocked unconscious.

Tom and Veka lifted their heads out of the pot, coughing, and then breathing with difficulty. They'd come close to drowning. Yet, such a dramatic method of switching species seemed oddly fitting to the wanderer's way of life—an appropriate welcome into the truculent world of magic.

Upon hearing Tom and Veka's screams, Alkefat, Darlith, Jake, and Blume rushed back as fast as they could. Fangas was lying on the ground while Tom and Veka were sitting with their faces and hair covered in broth and spices. Quickly, Alkefat and Shomes tied Fangas to a tree out of earshot while Darlith tended to Tom and Veka.

"Veka and I drank the potion after all," announced Tom. "I guess we will be joining you and your crazy wanderer ways. Who knows what we've gotten ourselves into," lamented Tom, moving closer to Veka before asking, "Are you okay, Veka?"

As Veka removed pieces of celery and various leaves and petals from her soaking-wet hair, she replied, "I'm okay. It all happened so fast." She was still confused and a bit dizzy. "I guess we'll get to see the world at a fast pace after all."

"Every corner of it," Tom replied with a soft smile.

"I didn't get a chance to ask what you wanted to do, Tom? Did you want to have magic?" asked Veka.

"It doesn't matter now. What matters is that we can be together no matter where we go."

They were both still shaken up.

"For what it's worth, I'm glad you both made it," stated Jake. "We're going to have so much fun!" Jake hugged Veka with his right arm and Tom with his left. "Oh, I almost forgot. I made something for you, Tom." Jake presented Tom with his hideous potato.

Tom looked at Jake's gift in disgust. "What is that thing?" he asked, moving slightly away from it.

"It's my first magical thing," Jake proudly declared, "and I'm giving it to you, Tom."

"Wow. Thanks. I feel so very yucky...I mean, lucky!" and they all laughed. Tom gently placed the potato on the ground, trying to forget he had ever seen it.

Veka got up and headed towards the lake, "I'm going in the water to wash. I'm sticky and smell like food."

"Good idea!" said Tom, following after her.

"Why not?" commented Jake. He, too, went in.

"Wait for me!" yelled Blume, running towards them.

While in the water, Veka spotted Kiel and Elath's brooms approaching. However, there was someone else on Kiel's broom. Darlith was watching but couldn't determine who was sitting behind Kiel... until she did. She froze for a moment, and then sprang into action. She grabbed the broom attached to her back and then launched a beam, hitting Menof right on the forehead. Menof fell into the water, knocked-out, about fifty feet away from Tom.

Elath smiled and looked at Kiel, who said, "Yeah, yeah...I should have anticipated that..." Kiel flew down and grabbed Menof by his tunic's neck section, as a mother dog would hold her new puppy, and then transported Menof to shore and laid him down on the beach.

"What is going on?" asked Darlith, agitated, "How is he not dead?"

A grunt came from Fangas, whose mouth was bound. He thought he'd never see his Brother again, yet there he was.

"He's a tough roach to kill," explained Elath. "Plus, he had help from Dazmian. For some reason, Dazmian believed Menof still had a purpose."

"What purpose could he possibly have?" Darlith asked.

"That's yet to be seen," answered Kiel. "For the time being, can we all agree not to kill him, please?"

Menof was lying down with his eyes closed as the kids came out of the water to look at the wizard that had caused so much trouble in everyone's life.

Kiel bent down to check Menof's pulse, "He's still alive, but it will take him a few minutes to regain consciousness." He turned towards Darlith and said, "I'm sorry you had to see Menof before I could explain." Kiel then described what Dazmian had put Menof through.

"I have a hard time believing he can change," said Darlith.

"We all do," confirmed Elath.

"I understand perfectly," Kiel agreed. "But what could one wizard do to five adult wanderers plus two newly added young members, right?" Kiel asked, referring to Jake and Blume.

"Make that four newly added young members," stated Tom.

"How do you mean?" inquired Kiel, looking first at Tom and then at the half-empty pot of potion. "What in the world happened here?" he exclaimed.

"Fangas happened here," answered Shomes, pointing towards the tree where Fangas was tied up, except... he wasn't there anymore.

"Where did he go?" exclaimed Alkefat.

"And where is Blume?" asked Veka.

# The Rat Hole

Menof opened his eyes in time to hear Fangas had taken Blume away.

"I'm afraid kidnapping runs in the family," Menof told them, rubbing the area hit by Darlith's beam on the left side of his head. "When my Uncle Beeny turned seven years old, he kidnapped one of his instructors for a few days because he wouldn't allow him to chew with his mouth open. My Father Servillius kidnapped a wizard that had created a potion he wanted that eliminated skin warts. My maternal Grandmother, granny Toots, that crooked-old mischief-maker, kidnapped a human child for a few years, a little boy who turned out remarkably rotten. And I, of course, kidnapped Darlith. So you see? It doesn't surprise me in the least."

"Really? That's the story you want to open with?" asked Jake.

"Where did Fangas take her?" Darlith demanded.

"How should I know? I just woke up from your blast, remember? But I'll be happy to help you find her," answered Menof, "Let me know if there's anything I can do."

"You're coming with us," stated Kiel.

"Let's split up to cover more ground," suggested Shomes.

"Agreed," said Elath.

They sorted themselves into groups. Alkefat and Jake together. Shomes took Tom. Kiel paired up with Menof. Darlith flew with Veka, and Elath traveled with Teal on her right shoulder.

"I don't suppose any of you knows where my broom went," asked Menof, but he received no answer as Shomes and Elath exchanged subtle grins.

"Let's reconvene here in about one hour. Hopefully, one of us will find them," stated Kiel.

Each group selected a different direction to begin their search. They looked high from the skies, watching for movement. They covered a large area, some following rivers, others flying over mountains, cruising on valleys, or zig-zagging through forest trees. Jake and Alkefat baked under the sun in an area full of dunes. They were thorough, yet time passed, and they had nothing to show for their effort.

Meanwhile, Fangas had dragged Blume for about a hundred yards, his right hand covering her mouth, until they were far enough from the others. He then carried her. The little girl weighed no more than forty pounds—a featherweight. The same could not be said about her personality; she had a fire inside her that burned as intensely as that of a tenacious witch. At six years old, Blume was fierce.

"I'm glad I'm going to get rid of you while you're still young," Fangas told Blume along the way. "As a grown-up, you might have become too resourceful." He wrestled with her while she tried to wiggle out of his arms. Unfortunately, her friends were too far away to hear the struggle.

Fangas had bound her hands and feet with the same string Shomes and Alkefat had used to restrain him. He had decided not to fly for fear he'd be easily spotted. He searched for a suitable place to hide and carry out his nefarious plan.

How do I get myself out of this? Blume thought, scared and frustrated. She looked around and located a butterfly. She focused on the insect with such intensity that the butterfly sensed someone watching it. Flying towards Blume, the graceful insect instantly understood that the girl was in trouble. Blume's little insect then hurried around, telling other butterflies what was happening. Pretty soon, a trail of flying, flapping wings followed Fangas at a safe distance until they got to a cave. Fangas entered the cave with Blume, and then put a spell on the entrance to create an invisible force field so no one could get in. Even though the butterflies were shut out, they refused to leave Blume's side. Unable to follow them inside, the insects gathered by the entrance until they covered it entirely.

Fangas let go of Blume's mouth, put her on the ground, and then tied her to a boulder.

Blume was shaking from fright. There she was again, with a most wretched wizard, captive in a cave. She tried to remember the spell she thought she used to get out of it the first time, but she was too nervous and anxious to come up with the right set of words. Under the circumstances, poetry seemed impossible.

"This is no place for creativity!" she screamed.

Fangas laughed. "Of all the things you could yell at me at this moment, this is what you choose to say?" He giggled. "Little girl, you are mad. Didn't I tell you I would kill you first? You knew what was coming to you."

"I haven't done anything to you," Blume protested. "What could a girl like me do to a wizard like you? This is an abuse of power!"

"What do you know about abuse of power?" he chuckled. "Do you even know what it means?"

"It means you're big, and I'm small, and it's not fair!" Blume yelled back.

"Guess what? The world isn't fair, and it's about time you learned that," Fangas countered. "I hate when little children are made to believe they live in a colorful dream world full of pink horses and candy clouds. The world is ugly, and I'm living proof of it."

"I agree," Blume stated, "uglier than Jake's potato."

"Jake's potato? What does that even mean?" asked Fangas, confused. "If you want to know why I want you gone, it's because Darlith truly cares about you. Darlith is why my Brother lost his mind and abandoned me," Fangas explained. "Darlith needs to pay for that. If you haven't noticed, I also don't like children, especially those with spunk. You're plenty sassy; you know that, right?" he inquired, lifting his right eyebrow.

"Let me out of here!" Blume screamed.

"I'm the only one who's getting out of here," replied Fangas. "The sooner you accept that, the better it will be for you."

He bent down to grab a couple of cockroaches, beetles, spiders, and one small rat. He gathered them in one hand and began chanting a spell. As soon as he finished, the critters turned into a single, shapeless blob. Seconds later, the lump fell out of Fangas' hand, and then grew, and grew, and grew into a large, bear-like animal Blume had never seen before.

The monster was dark brown, hairy, and rather toothy. Its tongue had the color and texture of a gigantic, overly-ripe strawberry. Its protruding eyes glowed in the dark in a dozen iridescent colors, and its ears looked like open holes that might lead directly into its brain. Its short, bushy tail was held up high such that its pink rear was, unfortunately, visible.

The nasty creature stared at Blume like she was the tastiest thing it had ever seen. It slowly moved towards her until its huge face was a mere few inches from hers. Blume closed her eyes and tried to move away, but she soon met the boulder behind her. The monster took a deep breath to absorb her scent, and then exhaled, showering her with a translucent, slimy mucus that discharged off its snout. The beast shook its head and roared like a famished lion cub. It wanted to eat Blume.

"You know how newborns are hungry right away?" asked Fangas. "All they can think of is food! Well, meet Davil, my new baby pet," Fangas said, pointing to the monster, "and it has to be fed. Can you take care of that for me, sweet Blume?" he asked, walking towards the exit. "Will you, hon?" he added with a diabolical, last glance back.

Fangas left the cave leaving the hungry creature alone with a tied-up, terrified Blume. In her despair, she wished Darlith would rush in, skidding to a stop right in front of her, coming to the rescue. But Blume also recalled a night when Tom talked about how important fire is to keep wild animals away. Then she remembered she'd taken Kiel's potion and recited the five Oaths. I must be at least a bit wanderer already, she thought. She closed her eyes so the beast wouldn't distract her from what she was about to do. In her mind, she pictured a wall of fire separating her from the beast.

Meanwhile, Davil inched forward as if savoring the thought of taking the first bite. It shuffled its paws slowly, stretching its neck, and placing its snout on her head. But as it opened its mouth to begin feasting, its paws caught on fire. Davil groaned in pain while stomping to put out the flames. It rolled to one side, and then the other, coating its legs with dirt and mud. It worked. After a few minutes, it had put out the fire. Its pain continued, however, and so did its howling and weeping. Davil dragged itself across the ground to a corner of the room to curl its now-hairless legs up into a fetal position. The beast stared at Blume, but this time not because she was delicious, but because it was terrified of her.

One hour after Kiel and company began searching for Blume, they all returned to Lake Sangress, frustrated by a sense of defeat. None of them had seen anything, not even the slightest clue of the path Fangas might have taken.

"I have a suggestion, if anyone cares to listen to me..." said Menof.

"Say whatever you have to say," answered Kiel.

"If I were trying to hide from a bunch of flying wanderers, I think I would hide underground," offered Menof.

"Of course you would, you little weasel," said Darlith, clenching her fists at the sound of Menof's voice.

"He has a point," said Kiel. "It's fair to say we panicked and took to the skies too fast. We should look for a trail on foot first. It's possible Blume left some clues behind."

"What if Fangas took Blume to his home in the Papuaka Islands?" asked Elath.

"That's possible, too," agreed Kiel. "How about Shomes and Alkefat go to Fangas' cave, and the rest of us look around here?"

"We can do that," answered Shomes.

Alkefat, Jake, Shomes, and Tom took off to look for Blume in the faraway islands. As they flew, Jake whined, "Do we really have to go to that dreadful place again?"

"What if Blume is held captive there?" yelled Tom from Shomes' broom.

"Yeah, yeah... but if I see pigeons again, I'm afraid I'll wet my pants," admitted Jake.

"We'll have to make a rest stop before we lose sight of land then," chuckled Shomes.

"Don't worry, I'll dump you in the ocean before you wet my broom," joked Alkefat, causing Shomes and Tom to giggle.

"But you bring up a good point," Alkefat added. "We need to get you all your own brooms as soon as possible. Plenty of padding, too; you'll crash a few times before you get a good handle on it."

"I flew by myself just fine on Elath's broom," pointed out Tom.

"You mean Elath's broom flew just fine with you on it!" explained Alkefat, chuckling with Shomes.

"There's such a thing as a rookie broom, Tom," added Shomes. "It took Kiel a few hours to fully control his new broom. I'd imagine it will take you longer."

"But Kiel told us that usually family members plant a tree and fill it with spells before one can have their own broom. Nobody did that for us. Where would our brooms come from?" asked Tom.

"We'll come up with something," said Alkefat.

"We're wanderers, remember?" said Shomes, "We can do almost anything you can think of!" he yelled while speeding up through the air.

Back at Lake Sangress, Kiel, Elath with Teal, Darlith, Veka, and Menof were canvassing the area. After a couple of minutes, they noticed a few broken twigs. They moved along to find cracked pine needles and dragging marks. Farther ahead, they came across crumbled leaves and even half a footprint on a mossy grass area along a path. But what finally tipped them off was Teal calling Elath with rapid sharp chirps and tweets full of excitement. Teal was surrounded by a cluster of butterflies that traveled around him as if following imaginary rings. But the cluster soon moved to greet Elath. At least ten butterflies circled her a few times before lining up in a straight line and flying ahead.

Darlith pointed out, "The butterflies will lead us to her!"

The six flew alongside the butterflies, meeting and collecting another hundred or so along the way until they came to a cave entrance. Thousands of butterflies of different sizes and patterns rested on what appeared to be an invisible layer covering the opening. When Elath and Darlith approached, the butterflies moved to the edges, forming a colorful arch around the entrance, like a trellis busting with blooming roses.

Upon close examination, Elath stated, "An energy field is blocking the way in."

Alas, Teal did not see this field, and in his eagerness to find Blume he launched himself full speed through the air, into the invisible barrier before anyone could do anything about it. The loudest THONK filled everyone's ears, and their hearts overflowed with sorrow. Teal had crashed into a wall he couldn't see with tremendous force. Few creatures could have survived. His tiny body, only a couple of inches in length, lay upside down on the ground with a broken neck.

Elath dropped to her knees by his side. "Nooo!" she yelled, tears cascading down her cheeks. She bent down further, looking for any signs of breathing. Nothing. She picked Teal up with both hands and pulled him close to her face. She cried. She kissed him. She cried.

Darlith and Kiel embraced Elath, one on each side, and then Veka joined in. The butterflies stopped batting their wings as a sign of respect. The heavy silence was the only sound available to accompany Elath's deepest sobs as if the forest itself stopped breathing for a moment.

And then a familiar voice called from inside the cave: "Darlith?"

"Blume?" Darlith exclaimed, standing up. She placed her right ear against the energy field to capture any other sound from within the cave's darkness.

"Darlith?" the voice called again.

"We're here, Blume!" Darlith yelled back, "We're coming to get you!"

Darlith took a few steps back and readied to blast the energy field. But Elath said, "Hold on a second, will you? Let us move out of the way first."

Elath placed Teal's little body inside her hood's pocket and moved with Kiel and Veka to the side.

Gently, Darlith blew air toward the butterflies as if asking them to step aside. The butterflies flew to nearby branches. Darlith shot a white beam straight toward the center of the field. No effect. Her beam did not even cause a tiny crack. Frustrated, she tried again but got the same result.

"This is going to take all of us, isn't it?" asked Elath.

"No problem," Kiel replied. "But it may be better to shoot to the side. We can make the opening bigger; the energy field won't cover the new section."

"Good idea," agreed Darlith.

Three white beams combined in the same spot, vaporizing the rock on impact. They moved their laser-like stream up and down along the edge of the opening until a hole big enough for them to pass through was cleared.

Darlith went in first, and she didn't have to go very far to find Blume. Still tied up, Blume wasn't hurt and appeared calm. Darlith picked her up in her arms and hugged her tight even before untying her from the boulder. "I'm so glad to see you," Darlith said.

"Not as glad as I am to see you," Blume replied, smiling. "Do you mind?" Blume asked, showing Darlith her bound hands.

"Not at all," Darlith replied, already working on releasing her.

Veka hugged Blume tight.

"Nice trick with the butterflies," complimented Kiel.

"Thank you," Blume answered politely, "but wait until I tell you what I did inside the cave; it was unbelievable!"

"Did Fangas hurt you?" asked Veka.

"At first, I was terrified. I thought I would die," admitted Blume, "but I realized I could protect myself."

As Blume explained the ordeal she'd just gone through, Kiel, Elath, Darlith, and Veka looked at the frightened, shivering creature coiled up in a dark corner of the cave. They hadn't noticed it before because Davil had been very quiet, hoping to be either undetected or ignored.

"Do you think Davil will ever return to being a mix of bugs and rodents?" Blume asked Kiel. "I feel bad for it. It wanted to eat me, but it was Fangas' fault. Fangas wanted to hurt Darlith."

"Let me take a look at him," replied Kiel. He stepped closer to Davil, and then petted the scared monster's head. "There, boy," Kiel soothed it as Davil's tight muscles relaxed. Kiel turned to Blume and said, "I can already feel him slowly shrinking. Fangas' incantation is, no doubt, temporary. It, or perhaps they, will be alright in a couple of hours. Hopefully they won't even remember what happened to them."

"But I will," countered Blume.

"I'm sure of it," Kiel responded. "You did well to use your powers. You're learning fast!"

"You sure are," added Elath. "Blume darling, do you know where Fangas went?"

"I don't know. I'm sorry...but I had other things on my mind," Blume replied.

"Of course," Elath concurred sympathetically. "You held your own, and I'm proud of you. Now, let's get out of here."

"I'll send word to Alkefat and Shomes that we found Blume, safe and sound," said Kiel. "I'll request that when they reach Papuaka Islands, they destroy all of Fangas' potions except the one that takes the magic away. I sense I'm not quite done with that one. But they should wait for Fangas to be out of his cave. I don't want them risking another confrontation—not yet, anyway. What's the fastest bird you can think of?" asked Kiel.

"If you get a peregrine falcon, you'd be in pretty good shape," replied Elath.

"Golden eagles are also amongst the fastest birds," added Darlith.

"Well, two are better than one," Kiel said, smiling. "Elath, please summon a peregrine falcon. Darlith, please summon a golden eagle. I'll put together messages for the birds to carry. I'll have Alkefat, Shomes, and the boys meet us at Castle Marmelo once they get the potion. There's much work ahead of us."

# Punishment or Vengeance

Elath, Darlith, Veka, Blume, and Menof were at Castle Marmelo's kitchen preparing lunch while having an animated discussion about what to do with Menof. Menof also had very specific opinions on the matter, which he voiced regardless of whether or not the others wanted to hear them.

"You could lock me up in a dark place filled with rats and forget about me," suggested Menof. "It's what I deserve. I promise I won't try to escape. Find my bones in a couple of years. Really, I don't mind; it seems like a fitting punishment."

"What's the point of punishing someone who does not mind being punished?" asked Veka. "We should find out what Menof minds, and then craft the punishment around that."

"You've all been talking about punishment, but it sounds more like vengeance," Menof pointed out.

"What's the difference between punishment and vengeance?" asked Blume.

"Vengeance, or revenge, supposedly gives the victims a sense of joy and satisfaction, although often that's not the case. Punishment is about facing the consequences of one's actions. Punishment can be geared toward the rehabilitation of the wrong-doer. It's also meant as a deterrent for the future," answered Darlith.

"If vengeance is what you seek, then it's easy: kill me," continued Menof.

"As good as that sounds," said Elath, "killing outside of battle is beneath us, especially killing a prisoner. I'm still trying to figure out how much of a threat you are."

"I'm not a prisoner anymore," replied Menof. "I'm sitting in your kitchen, without restraints of any kind, having a friendly conversation. You have become comfortable with the idea that I don't want to run away or hurt you. You believe I am a different wizard than I was before. It's only a matter of time before someone offers me some tea!"

"Perhaps," said Elath, "but I have to tell you, I don't know whom I dislike more, a bad Menof or a good one."

They all chuckled.

Alkefat, Shomes, and the boys came flying through the window.

"What's so funny?" asked Shomes.

"Oh, not much," answered Darlith. "We're simply discussing how to make Menof suffer. Alas, it seems nothing will make the new Menof suffer. He has already accepted whatever gruesome fate we might choose for him."

"According to Kiel, Menof had a horrible time during his transformation," explained Elath.

"I can attest to that," confirmed Menof. "Sadly, I remember everything."

"Speaking of Kiel, where is he?" asked Alkefat.

Blume answered right away. "He went to the living room. He looked tired."

"More like worried, I would say," added Veka.

Tom and Jake sat around the kitchen table anticipating a meal, while Alkefat, followed by Shomes, left the kitchen looking for Kiel. He was sitting on a leather couch in the massive living room, looking pensive. Shomes and Alkefat sat on two chairs around the heavy, stone coffee table.

Alkefat held a bottle full of brown liquid. "Here's the potion you requested," Alkefat said, handing the bottle to Kiel. "I hope you didn't want the whole pot—it was enormous! I brought you a good-sized sample instead."

"This is plenty, for now, Alkefat. Thank you," replied Kiel, grabbing the bottle.

"We destroyed the rest," added Shomes. "Luckily, I found several books filled with scribbled potions, and I'm confident you can find the recipe there. Fangas had the books hidden." Shomes giggled at the thought.

If there was a hiding place that had been written about, talked about, or thought about, Shomes knew about it. It's how he got the job as Guardian of the Library in the first place. Finding hidden things, as well as hiding them, was his strong suit. Shomes could, somehow, sense concealed things, as if they emitted a signal at just the right frequency for Shomes to pick up.

"We're fortunate indeed," said Kiel. "You all did very well." He then went back to looking pensive.

Kiel was preoccupied with how to protect his loved ones—as well as the world—from Fangas. But how do I restrain Fangas' powerful magic? he wondered. It would be tough to contain such an able wizard. He turned towards Shomes to ask, "Is there a prison, a cage even, anywhere in the world, strong enough to keep Fangas locked up?"

"If there is, I don't know it," Shomes replied. "The Highest Wanderer Council keeps the most wanted, wicked wanderers under constant surveillance. There was a time when evil wanderers were incarcerated, but sooner or later, they all managed to escape their prison. If there is one thing they all have in common, it is an extraordinary ability for scheming. They're all escape artists! The Council decided to enlist the help of enchanted animals to shadow them. At any given point, a known wicked wanderer might be guarded by a combination of a dozen trained magical animals and two wanderer guards. They are followed wherever they go and stopped if they try to stir up trouble. It's a difficult task, but there's no way around it. The Council concluded these wanderers were unfit to have magic, and yet they had no way of preventing them from misusing it other than through constant supervision."

"Is that so?" Kiel wondered out loud. He turned to Alkefat. "If I gave you Fangas' potion to temporarily take the magic away, do you think you could figure out a way to make it permanent?"

Alkefat laughed. "By using wanderer and human flesh and bones like Fangas suggested? Who's going to volunteer?" He chuckled.

Ever since he was little, Alkefat belonged in his kitchen with his odd, hand-made utensils, deformed, over-used pots, incomprehensibly sharp gadgets, and colorful, foul-smelling, often gooey ingredients. He also belonged in his library with his beloved cooking books. Surrounded by his equipment, big and small, he was happy. He thrived! It would be a fabulous way to spend his time—a rejuvenating experience!

As the thought of becoming the wizard who denied magic powers to those who didn't deserve them filled Alkefat's mind, he became more and more excited. What a legacy! He pondered, eyes shining bright. But then it dawned on him: That wouldn't be his legacy but Kiel's. Kiel is the chosen one, the one Dazmian entrusted with protecting the wanderers of the Earth. The one who will ensure Fangas, and others like him, will be taken care of. He's young, bright, and determined. A spell or potion of that magnitude required knowledge that Alkefat did not possess. Kiel will find a way, Alkefat was certain.

"The good news, Kiel, is that I know exactly who can help you," stated Alkefat.

"Really? Who?" asked Kiel, excited.

"You," said Alkefat, pointing his wrinkly-thin, slightly-bent index finger at Kiel.

Shomes couldn't help but giggle at the dilemma Kiel and Alkefat were in, with each believing the other was in the best position to neutralize Fangas.

"What are you talking about?" replied Kiel, confused. "If I knew how to stop Fangas for good, I wouldn't have asked you in the first place."

"You may not know how to do it now, and that's your challenge—to figure it out," said Alkefat. "Think about it, Kiel. You have been shown the books of knowledge. What better tool to use against villains?"

"Alkefat's right," agreed Shomes. "The content of the books might not make sense to you now, but if you spend some time by yourself, stewing on it, meditating, fermenting all the information and wisdom they contain, I believe you will find the answers you're looking for."

"I suppose it makes sense...even if I can't see it now," said Kiel, trying to keep an open mind about it. If Alkefat and Shomes thought he could do it, it was worth a try.

"You have been thrust into some pretty big responsibilities, Kiel," continued Alkefat, "and I'm sorry it happened so fast. But I don't think we have a choice. Fangas is mad and capable. In his effort to have everyone love him, he's become a most hated wizard. His behavior is erratic, ill-advised, destructive, and vindictive. He has the power to do so much damage! To cause so much grief!"

"Yes, I hear you loud and clear, Alkefat. Shomes is right, too. I have to think this through for a while on my own," concluded Kiel, leaving the room.

In the hallway, Kiel ran into Darlith, who asked for half a cup of Fangas' potion to give Menof so that he could be left unattended overnight. Kiel poured enough in Darlith's mug and walked towards his bedroom. He spent the rest of the day meditating on his bed, figuring out what it all meant and how to put it together.

He had memorized every page of the Book of Deadlies and the Book of Deltas, but that didn't mean he understood them. The Book of Deadlies contained the deadliest spells that the wisest wanderers, over thousands of years, were able to create. It was written in Obslij, the most powerful language that ever existed.

Obslij was the language of Earth's history, one that combined all possible ways of communication between living and non-living things. It had such accumulated wisdom and energy that no other language could match it. Obslij had absorbed millions of years of evolution of a fully sentient planet, with all its oceans, land mass, atmosphere, plants, and animals, including humans and wanderers, inside it. This primordial language also encompassed planetary communication, especially from nearby galaxies.

The Book of Deltas allowed wanderers access to those spells, serving as a translation for future generations. The Books ensured that chosen wanderers could continue developing potent concoctions to confront new challenges that might endanger the planet's health and that of its inhabitants. It was of utmost importance that the Books were hidden and protected. The consequences of them falling into the wrong hands would be devastating. The itty-bitty, wicked hands, of a minute wanderer, on a tiny planet, of a little star system, within a small galaxy, could affect the whole of the Universe.

At first, Kiel had been overwhelmed by the assignment, so he did the only thing he knew to do when presented with something so enormous: take one step at a time.

Every word he read in the Book of Deadlies had to be translated first for him to understand. Translating it was not easy, given the little time he had been able to devote to studying Obslij, but he hoped if he put his mind to it, he would make good progress.

In his mind, he opened both Books at the same time. This fact allowed him, somehow, to understand Obslij better. The Book of Deadlies' pages were covered in gold and silver accents that highlighted the importance of the text. The first spell on page two of this thick, sacred book appeared to be a training exercise with two different possible endings to choose from. The elaborate, ancient, brightly colored drawings indicated that this particular spell was meant to kill a lion. The scene depicted was that of a mad lion that had walked into an African village full of kids at play. The lion would be forced into a deep sleep using the first ending. With the alternative ending, however, the only thing left of the lion was skin and fur. Its insides were vaporized.

But I'm not in Africa, and I don't know where to find a lion around here, Kiel thought. I could find a mountain lion; would the spell work in that case? He decided to continue reading.

Page four of the Book of Deadlies contained a spell designed to eliminate a devastating plague of locusts. Kiel slowly translated it as

*Kill the locusts in the field*
*Let the land be fully healed*
*Turn them into fertilizer*
*Be the best crop energizer.*

There was a second part to the spell, but Kiel had trouble translating it. He continued browsing the Book of Deadlies in his mind, looking for anything that would indicate how to make a temporary formula permanent.

He began translating the titles of the spells only, which, together with the illustrations, could give him an idea of the kinds of things they could do. Some incantations could assassinate wanderers remotely. Others could move planets and stars as if the Universe was a mind-bogglingly large game of marbles. Turning page after page, he became increasingly discouraged until he came across page fifty, entitled "Tips."

Tip number one was this: "Do not taste or ingest these concoctions."

"Well, duh," he murmured. He wondered why such tips were not at the beginning of the book instead, but then he figured it was an extra layer of complexity added to discourage less determined wizards.

The second tip talked about the need to protect one's hands and face when preparing dangerous potions, stating that many talented wanderers had been lost because they were too impatient to follow this simple step. The third tip was also safety-related, regarding handling fire, dynamite, and other explosives.

But it was tip number nine that finally gave him what he needed. It described how some wanderers could create powerful, temporary incantations but were unaware of what it takes to make them permanent. It spoke of a wizard who tricked a mad hyena into drinking a poisonous potion. The hyena supposedly died, only to attack the wizard three hours later. The text explained that, in most cases, all it takes is to burn a mix of finely ground chalk and clay until the carbon dioxide is removed from the mixture. Once this prepared blend is added to a potion, its effects become permanent enough so that the intended target does not recover for a long time, if ever. The tip cautioned the reader that a small quantity is sufficient to reach the desired goal and that too much mixture could ruin the consistency of the potion, possibly turning it into a solid, especially if left unattended for a few hours. The last sentence of tip nine offered the following insight: "Depending on the quantity added, it may have an undesired impact on taste (see tip number one)."

"Got it," said Kiel, closing the book in his mind. "I can assure you," he said as if talking to an imaginary Dazmian, "I have no intention of trying the potion on my own body!"

But then he realized giving the potion to Fangas would be a problem. Fangas was undoubtedly not going to take it voluntarily.

Kiel fell asleep, exhausted.

# The Plan

The next day, at an entirely too early an hour, Kiel woke up with a plan. He was happy to see Alkefat and Shomes had spent the night at the castle, as their shoes were neatly arranged next to the kitchen's fireplace. He brewed a fresh pot of loose-leaf green tea, and then peeled and sliced five fresh brown pears from Elath's garden. He then cut up cheese and bread and put them on the kitchen dining table.

Kiel walked around the castle, knocking on bedroom doors, waking everyone up, "Wakey Wakey! The sun is shining!" he yelled loud enough to be heard through the thick wooden doors.

His efforts were met with unhappy grunts. Shomes politely asked Kiel to go away forever, while Elath threw one of her boots, hitting the door with a loud thunk, and then pulled her heavy purple velvet blanket back over her head. But a few minutes later, Alkefat, Shomes, Darlith, and Elath gathered in the kitchen, and Kiel served breakfast to them with a smile they were not necessarily happy to see.

"Why would you wake us up this early, Kiel?" asked Elath. "I was only in my fourth dream," she added sleepily.

"Go ahead and start eating. I will tell you as soon as your stomachs are not empty," he replied.

Kiel explained he'd found a way to take Fangas' magic away for good. But once his audience began to cheer, he cautioned, "Not so fast. We still have to figure out how to deliver it to him."

Menof, who had been listening just long enough behind the closed kitchen door, stepped in. "I can help you with that. My Brother trusts me."

"Why would you help us?" asked Kiel.

"Because I owe you a debt bigger than life itself," Menof replied. "I'm prepared to die if that's what it takes. I've seen and heard what Fangas can do, what he's become, or what he always was, but I was too stupid to see."

"Well, well, well..." said Alkefat, pensive. "Maybe this is what Dazmian meant when he said Menof can be useful."

"You're not going to die, Menof... unless your Brother decides to kill you," replied Kiel. "We need to trick Fangas into taking the potion. How do you think we can do that?" Kiel posed this question to everyone.

"How much of it do you think he needs to take?" asked Darlith.

"I would say a minimal amount, now that it's a permanent blend," said Kiel.

"If it's a small amount... I have an idea that might work," said Shomes.

"In that case, shouldn't we notify the Council about our intentions?" asked Alkefat.

"We will...after we're through with it," answered Kiel. "But don't worry, our actions are more than justified. Fangas is a murderer who has driven our species to the brink of extinction. By taking his powers away, he's getting off easy."

"Very well," said Shomes, "here's what I'm thinking..."

# Growing Powers, Growing Pains

It was a sunny, breezy morning in Verdeval. As Tom and Jake woke up in Tom's room, they got startled by each other's eyes.

"Tom, I don't want you to freak out about this, but you have a ring around your eyes that you didn't have before," said Jake, pointing to Tom's eyes with his right index finger and drawing an imaginary circle in the air.

"I'm guessing it's quite similar to the one you have around yours," replied Tom.

"Do I?" Jake jumped off the floor mattress and rushed towards the small mirror located over an old chest of drawers. "Would you look at that?" Jake exclaimed, "It's beautiful! So this is what wanderers look like, huh? I wonder if Veka and Blume have it too."

"Probably," answered Tom.

"How are we going to hide it from our parents?" asked Jake.

"Good question," answered Tom, pensive. "It's possible they can't see it since we didn't notice it in Elath and the others."

"I hope you're right, because it would be hard to explain. I'd like to know if we can do more magical things. Kiel said our powers will grow over time."

"Well, you already know how to grow potatoes, so how about growing some bacon and eggs to give me a proper breakfast?" suggested Tom.

Jake replied by starting a pillow fight that ended, after many laughs, in an entirely messy bedroom.

"We better clean this up before anyone else sees it," warned Tom.

Afterwards, Tom and Jake went downstairs for breakfast, avoiding eye contact with their parents in case they could notice the change. They ate quickly and then went outside to explore their new skills.

Heading towards the barn, Jake asked, "What should we try first?"

"I don't know... Remember Blume said she was able to make fire just by thinking about it? I'd love to try that!" replied Tom. "What would you like to try, Jake?"

"Hmm, Alkefat did a funny trick using bugs as puppets; maybe I'll try that."

Inside the barn, two cows, a horse, and several free-roaming chickens ignored their presence.

"Call me crazy, Tom, but I don't think you should start a fire inside a barn."

"Don't worry, if it works, I'll put it out right away," replied Tom. "Our attempts need to happen behind closed doors. Or do you want to risk being seen?"

"I do not."

They both sat on the ground; Tom sat with his back to the barn door and Jake right across from him. Tom grabbed a few hay sticks and bunched them, placing them between himself and Jake. Jake corralled a couple of beetles and put them on the ground to his right side.

"Should we start?" Tom asked.

"I'm ready," said Jake.

With eyes closed, Tom thought about lighting the hay sticks on fire while Jake thought about lifting the beetles. After a few minutes of silence, they opened their eyes.

"Anything?" Asked Tom looking around.

"Not that I can see. Everything is as it was before."

"Bummer!" exclaimed Tom, snapping his fingers.

Suddenly, Tom's hay sticks caught on fire.

"Wow, wow, wow, put it out, Tom! You'll scare the animals!"

As soon as Jake said that, the two cows, the horse, and the chickens began to levitate a few inches off the ground. All the animals in the barn complained as loud as they could. The cows mooed in anger, the horse neighed in fear, and the chickens cackled and squawked, running and crashing into each other in total confusion.

Tom threw sand over the fire, quickly putting it out. But bringing the animals back down was a different story.

Hearing the commotion from the house, Tom's Dad ran towards the barn, yelling, "What in the world is happening over there?"

Tom saw his Dad approach through a hole in the barn door. "Get the animals down, Jake! My Dad's coming!"

"And how am I supposed to do that?"

"I don't have a clue!" yelled Tom, "but you better hurry up!"

Jake turned to the animals and commanded, "Down!"

No effect.

"Down!" Jake yelled even louder, although he could hardly be heard over the animal's screams.

Jake fell to his knees and implored, "Would you please come down?"

The animals touched down and immediately went quiet as if nothing had happened.

Mr. Wellson opened the door, "What on Earth is going on here?" he asked. "Why were the animals so upset?"

Tom was speechless. Luckily, Jake was not. "A swarm of bees came in and scared them," answered Jake. "But as soon as the bees left, the animals calmed down." Jake's ability to lie was perfect for covering up magical disasters.

"Well, well, well," said Mr. Wellson, looking around. "That was something, wasn't it? It does smell a bit like fire, though..."

"I think it's just the animals' fear, sir," answered Jake.

"Animal fear smells like fire?" asked Mr. Wellson skeptically. "What are the two of you doing here anyway? I trust you wouldn't put the animals in danger, right?"

"Of course not, sir," answered Jake.

"And what's with you, Tom? Has the cat got your tongue?" asked Mr. Wellson.

"What cat?" asked Tom, too shaken to think straight.

"Tell you what, both of you go clean the pig stalls. You seem to have too much time on your hands," Mr. Wellson instructed.

Tom and Jake humbly and slowly walked toward the pig stalls.

"On the bright side," said Tom, "our attempt wasn't completely unsuccessful."

"Yeah... but I think we could use a bit more guidance..."

# Oh, Brother!

Menof was ready. He'd gone over Shomes' plan in detail and even rehearsed it several times in front of a full-length mirror in the bedroom he was allowed to sleep in at the castle. His performance had to be totally convincing. All that was left to do was to find Fangas.

"I can help with that too," Menof had assured the others. "Papuaka Islands are Fangas' home, but not his only hideout. He has a place up in the mountains with a gorgeous view of one of the greatest lakes in the area. He loves fishing there, and one time he caught a forty-pound trout he was very proud of. It's his vacation cave."

Kiel had asked Alkefat to stay behind to organize and catalog all of Fangas' potions and spells contained in the books Shomes had found. Alkefat had already done more than enough to help, and it was time for him to dedicate himself to what he liked best: meddling with potions.

Darlith would help Alkefat with that task. She didn't mind sitting this fight out, as she was still exhausted from all the physical and emotional turmoil she had endured in her life.

Blume, too, had decided to stay at the castle because she still vividly remembered her ordeal with Fangas and Davil the day before. She begged Veka to stay with her so they could play with Belugo and Mint while swimming in Elath's lake. Veka agreed.

Jake couldn't go. His Mom requested that he take care of his baby Sister while Mrs. Hellington visited her husband in jail. After that, Jake's Mom planned to go to Verdeval's church to join the choir, fulfilling her long-time dream of singing. Even though Jake wanted to be by Tom's side when they confronted Fangas one last time, he couldn't let his Mom down at this sensitive time.

Kiel, Elath, Shomes, Menof, and Tom went after Fangas. After all, Shomes' plot involved only three main characters: Menof, Elath, and Tom. The rest would be there to deal with any eventuality should things not go according to plan.

Fangas' vacation lake was enormous, about twenty-two miles long and twelve miles wide. It held trillions of gallons of water, fed by the snow gathered in the majestic surrounding mountains. Of the numerous sandy beaches available to land on, they selected a small one on the southern tip of the lake.

Tom couldn't resist dipping his hands and feet in the lake. The water was clear and frigid, as freshly melted snow would be, but he didn't seem to mind it.

Kiel stayed back in the forest, preparing the permanent mixture and adding it to Fangas' brown potion. This was just a precaution so Menof wouldn't learn how to do it. Once the potion was ready, Kiel approached Menof and said, "It's time. Are you sure you want to do this?"

"I'm sure," replied Menof.

"Very well, then," said Kiel, pouring enough drops of the potion to coat Menof's lips thoroughly. A few drops made it into Menof's mouth.

"It tastes terrible!" complained Menof, resisting the impulse to wipe it off and spit. "I'm glad a little bit is sufficient."

"I believe you." Kiel smiled. "Now, Menof, try to do any spell you can think of."

Menof pondered for a few seconds, and then remembered a spell he loved as a young wanderer. He walked towards the lake and scooped up about a cup and a half of water in his hands. He began:

> Liquid water play this game
>
> Turn to snow from which you came
>
> Cool my hands so I can build
>
> A little snowman nice and chilled.

But the water, instead of freezing up, slowly trickled out of Menof's callous hands. A little tear fell off Menof's left eye as the gravity of what had just happened sank in. Menof no longer had magic.

"It works," Menof said, hiding his teary eyes from the others. "We can proceed with the plan."

Elath bound Menof's hands behind him. Then Elath, Tom, and Menof sat down on the sand to wait. Kiel gave the potion to Elath, and then he and Shomes retreated to a hidden area in the forest where they could still see them.

It wasn't too long before pigeons began circling above their heads. Looking up at them, Elath said, "Fangas will be here shortly."

Sure enough, Fangas showed up ten minutes later. He came in, launching strike after strike toward Elath. He was determined to free Menof once and for all.

"How dare you mistreat my Brother!" Fangas screamed from the sky, flying swiftly, attacking from many angles as he zigzagged along.

"Fangas! Help me!" Menof shouted.

Tom ran back to take cover behind nearby rocks. Elath defended herself with strikes from her broom, "I came here to finish you and your Brother in battle!" she screamed back.

"And where are your friends, Elath? Why did you only bring one of your pets?" asked Fangas.

"Tom is enough to keep me company, and I can defeat you by myself. You know me, Fangas, I take matters into my own, capable hands!" She launched a beam that struck the front tip of Fangas' broom, destabilizing him for a few seconds.

"Then untie Menof. Don't you want a fair fight?" Fangas yelled, getting closer to them.

At that moment, one of Fangas' strikes hit Elath's left arm. The hit spun her around, and she fell, face down, on top of Menof. Elath took the potion she had hidden in her chest and spread a few fresh drops around Menof's lips. She stood up, ran towards Tom, and they disappeared into the woods together.

"Run, coward, run!" screamed Fangas.

Fangas landed next to Menof and began to untie him, while Menof said, "At last," with great relief.

When Fangas finished untying Menof's hands, Menof turned around, and Fangas saw Menof no longer had an optis surrounding the iris in his eyes.

"What have they done to you, Menof?" Fangas asked, concerned. "Your eyes have lost the optis!"

Menof grabbed Fangas' head with two hands and kissed his lips. Fangas pushed Menof away...but it was too late. Fangas felt something inside of him was seriously wrong as if part of his life force was leaving his body. He struggled to comprehend. Looking into Menof's eyes, he said, "Oh, Brother! What have you done?" as the bright iridescence of his optis disappeared.

# Broom Ceremony

K iel's tree had a name that hung from the lowest branch on a wooden sign in beautiful, slanted letters. It read "Sarbol." Sarbol was truly splendid. It stood out in beauty, size, and health. Its massive canopy was full of large, dark green leaves. Its trunk, a phenomenal seven feet in diameter, was covered in smooth, dark bark that appeared to scream, "Hug me!" And that's precisely what the kids did. Tom, Veka, Blume, and Jake could barely hide their enthusiasm as they were about to get their brooms.

Kiel approached Sarbol and placed his forehead and both hands on it. He had to deliver the news to the tree. In his mind, Kiel spoke to Sarbol and explained that they needed four branches for the new four members of the wanderer community. Even though Sarbol was a relatively young tree of only seventeen years of age, it had all the wisdom Ottah had been able to impart to it and the wisdom acquired through the ground, plants, animals, and atmosphere around it. The request was a lot to ask of a tree in one day, given that a standard broom ceremony only involved one branch. Afterwards, Kiel warned everyone to back off to give Sarbol enough space to do what needed to be done.

Four branches, each about six feet long and three inches thick, fell with a considerable amount of noise, as if a cluster of thunder strikes was upon them, slightly shaking the ground beneath them—an incredible gift from a magnificent creature.

Alkefat began reciting a spell to help the tree seal the injuries created by the release of the branches. The tree could better protect itself from bacteria and fungi that might otherwise damage it, and it would allow new growth around each sealed wound.

> *Isolate!*
>
> *A barrier create*
>
> *Seal!*
>
> *It's your way to heal*
>
> *Grow!*
>
> *Around each blow*
>
> *Bloom!*
>
> *After birthing a broom*
>
> *Thank you!*
>
> *From this humble crew.*

Elath and Darlith assigned the branches to the kids and provided them with carving knives so they could begin shaping them. Shomes volunteered to add the end-brushes and the final touches for extra smoothness and straightness. Afterwards, they would all have a picnic under Sarbol's shade.

But the best part was still ahead of them. Elath had prepared an area in the backyard for broom races. She wouldn't allow the kids to stop racing until they became experienced riders. The kind that don't fall off the broom while being attacked, at full speed, by pigeons as they fly over the smoke and explosions of an erupting volcano. Because that was simply unacceptable!